Other Books in the Adventures of David and the Magic Coin Series

Leonardo da Vinci, Columbus, and Little David
Michelangelo, Columbus, and Little David
Henry VII, Prince Arthur, Columbus, and Little David
Anne of Brittany, Arnaud the Page, and Little David
Isabella of Spain, Boabdil, Columbus, and Little David

Riding a Buffalo with Theodore Roosevelt and Sitting Bull

The Adventures of Little David and the Magic Coin

Pauline de Saint-Just Gross

A Historical Novel

ISBN: 153369947X
ISBN 13: 9781533699473
Library of Congress Control Number: 2016909666
CreateSpace Independent Publishing Platform
North Charleston, South Carolina

Idea David Gross
Associate Editor Michelle Gross
Book Cover Mark Harmon
Edited by Lora Bolton CS

By Invitation only

To All Curious Children who love to learn

Ride a buffalo. Ride a canoe.

There's plenty of fun to be had!

Dance with the Sioux. Pet a bobcat.

You are invited to join us on this amazing trip.

Who:	The Lakota and Theodore Roosevelt
Where:	Little Eagle Village, South Dakota
When:	September 15, 1883
What:	Celebrating the Lakota way of life

All you need to bring is a huge appetite for learning and a willingness to savor the thrills of the adventure.

Hope you join us,

David and Michelle

Contents

Prologue

This is how David's adventure started...

On his way to school one day, David finds an old coin. He can't help playing with it while his teacher, Mrs. Savant, talks about Christopher Columbus. He wishes he could travel with him rather than just hear about him. That's when he discovers the coin's magic.

David will find himself in the company of some of the most amazing people in history.

In 1491, David is face to face with Columbus, who is looking for ways to fulfill his dream of finding a new trade route from Europe to Asia.

With Columbus, David meets Leonardo da Vinci, the famous painter and inventor, and while visiting his workshop, he befriends Salai, his mischievous and naughty apprentice. Salai leads David on an exciting journey through the workshop, where each room houses extraordinary inventions. Along the way, David learns to dissect frogs and make dye from a flower—discovering secrets of da Vinci's art in the process. And finally, he gets to take part in one of the inventor's greatest experiments.

With a map given to Leonardo da Vinci, Columbus heads to Florence to meet the greatest banker of his time, Lorenzo de Medici, who he is hoping will finance his dream voyage.

Florence is celebrating de Medici, who is their ruler. David joins a parade of revelers. Amid the crowd, he meets a beautiful little girl, a troublemaking monkey, and a young artist named Michelangelo. Michelangelo will lead him through the city of Florence and the Medici gardens, teaching him about the beauty of life in Florence and the magical ability of art to bring stone to life.

Lorenzo is very busy with Florence's problems. Dissatisfied, Columbus leaves.

Still hoping to find a king willing to finance his search for a new trade route to Asia, Columbus, with David tagging along, goes to London, England, where Henry VII rules. David and Henry's son Prince Arthur quickly become friends, playing on the royal barge as it floats down the River Thames. David learns about British history, but the two boys flirt with danger when they play too close to the dragon-shaped cannon on the prow of the barge. Safe on land, the boys take part in a most extraordinary celebration the king holds for the birth of his new son, Prince Henry. David gets to ride a jeweled elephant and a serious camel, watches morality plays based on the lives of nine famous people from history, and attends an amazing fete where live birds fly out of pies. Henry VII is busy building his kingdom and suggests that Columbus visit France.

On to France, they go to a brutal arrival. David comes face to face with a massive, angry-looking wild boar. But just as the boar lunges, he is saved by none other than King Charles VIII of France. When the king puts Arnaud in charge of David, the two boys become coconspirators in a plot to hide a baby rabbit from the hunting dogs. Back at the castle, motherly Queen Anne of Brittany wants David to learn about Renaissance France's court life. With Arnaud as his guide, David explores the castle, visiting the scriptorium, the buttery, and the bell tower and gleefully exploring a maze of secret passageways. Along the way, David learns about calligraphy from a monk, discovers how wine is made, and engages in knightly games, including jousting and archery. All the while, Columbus is trying very hard to convince Charles VIII to finance his trip. Charles VIII just got married and needs time to think about it.

Columbus decides to go see Queen Isabella in Spain. They arrive just after the Muslim sultan Boabdil surrenders the rule of Granada to the Catholic monarchs, Ferdinand and Isabella. While many are celebrating, David finds himself alone and in danger as he encounters stampeding bulls. Rescued by Boabdil, David becomes a guest at the Alhambra, a magical red palace filled with twelfth-century inventor Al Jazari's amazing robotic inventions. David befriends the Moorish king's son Ahmed, and the two explore the castle together. But soon, David asks Boabdil to take him to Queen Isabella so he can rejoin Columbus. When the sultan and his son take David to the queen's compound, however, they might be stepping into a trap...and David only makes matters worse when he asks one too many questions.

But the magic coin saves him and he finds himself back in the classroom, sitting and listening to Mrs. Savant.

1

The Museum's Winking Indian

"Look at the Indian standing by Theodore Roosevelt," David said excitedly, jumping out of the New York taxi stopped in front of the museum. "He winked at me."

"Come on, David!" Michelle shouted, laughing. "You know the Indian didn't wink. You made that up!"

"Well, let's go check it out," David said, already on the steps leading up to the museum.

Michelle, curious as ever, wanted to see if David was telling the truth about the impressive Indian standing by Theodore Roosevelt, the twenty-sixth president of the United States. She ran after him.

"Hey, you two, wait a minute while I pay the cab!" shouted Lizzie, nervously looking for change in her purse to give the impatient New

York taxicab driver. "Don't go anywhere! We need to wait for your cousins, Amber and Derrick."

David didn't listen to his babysitter. He ran up to the statue of Theodore Roosevelt.

"This is incredible; we are here at the American Museum of Natural History. Did you know Theodore Roosevelt had a museum in his bedroom?" David asked Michelle, his cousin and best friend. "He loved animals and was a big collector just like me."

"I know," Michelle said, unimpressed. She was running up the stairs after David, who was already at the imposing statue of the Indian standing by Roosevelt right in front of the museum. "Mrs. Savant, our teacher, told us."

Michelle looked carefully at the Indian, who was wearing a headdress and a bear-claw necklace. "He is as stiff as stone," Michelle said, after meticulously studying the statue. "He couldn't wink. You always exaggerate."

"No, I don't. And I will prove it to you," David said, picking up a gray and white feather he had found under the Indian statue. He quickly put it in his curly blond hair. "How about this feather?" the blue-eyed boy asked wittily, pointing at the feather. "Where do you think it came from?"

"The pigeons walking on the sidewalk," replied the pretty, perky brown-haired girl with two long ponytails and dark-brown eyes, cleverly pointing to the pigeons nearby.

"Sometimes, you are no fun. Use your imagination," David said and added, "With the eagle feather in my hair, I am now an Indian."

"How about me?" asked Michelle.

"You're an Indian too," replied David. "Aren't you wearing wampum around your neck?"

"Yes," Michelle said, touching the beautiful seed-and-shell necklace she had worked so hard at making for Mrs. Savant, her history teacher. She had told them not to miss the best museum in the world, the American History Museum when visiting New York City.

"There you go," David replied. "That makes you an ad interim Indian too."

"*Ad interim* Indian, heh?" Michelle said.

"A temporary Indian," David replied.

"I am not dumb," Michelle said. "I know what *ad interim* means."

David put his hand to his mouth, flapping his hand on and off as he uttered the vocal sound "Wowowowo" and danced clockwise around the statues to Michelle's dismay.

"I am so embarrassed," Michelle said. "Everyone is looking at us."

"Well, come on," David told Michelle. "Don't stand there; dance with me. Pretend we are thanking Wakan Tanka, the Great Spirit, for being here."

"Are you crazy? Dance around a statue in front of all these people. I don't want to be laughed at," she said, crossing her arms. "I'll watch you from a distance."

"OK," David said.

"I'll only dance with *real* Indians in an Indian village," Michelle added defiantly, knowing it was impossible.

David stopped dancing, pulled Michelle close to him gently, and mumbled something.

2

Where Are We?

Michelle and David were now skipping and hopping behind untroubled and happy Indians who were dancing in a circle to the sound of the drums, totally oblivious to the presence of the two unusually dressed children. It was as if they were invisible.

"What happened? Where are we?" Michelle asked, noticing she was surrounded by energetic Indian women and men, zigzagging, stomping, and shuffling their feet in a circle while other Indian men were sitting around the circle playing drums. Some had their faces painted; others were wearing animal skins and animal masks. Colorful feathers adorned their hair or their masks. They were wearing arm and ankle bands and colorful braids. They all seemed happy. The smell of burning sage was making it a unique experience.

"A Sioux Indian village," David answered. "Mrs. Savant was just teaching us about the Lakota

Indians, who lived in South Dakota. Lakota means *friends*. So, we will be OK here. She said Indians had a dance for everything. Remember she showed us a video of a lively but peaceful dance meant to ask for the village's well-being. Maybe this is what this dance is about."

"What's that smell?" Michelle asked.

"The Lakota used herbs in their ceremony, such as sage," David answered. "Mrs. Savant talked about that too."

"How did we get here?" Michelle asked, overwhelmed by the scene in front of her. She was trying to understand how they had gotten there and what they were doing among Indian women and men, dancing, while children in the background were observing their elders.

"It must have been the dance we did around the statues." David snickered. "It must have been *magic*."

"Magic?" Michelle replied skeptically. "Maybe..." She laughed. "Maybe it was the feather."

"Why are you laughing?" David asked, grinning. "How do you know it wasn't?"

He knew how they had gotten there, but he would not share that secret just yet.

David smiled, holding on to his magic coin. *My coin still has power*, he thought. *I traveled with Christopher Columbus wishing on my coin, and now we are here in an Indian village.*

"Why are these bizarre skulls on the ground?" Michelle asked, pointing. "They look scary with the horns."

"You forgot that too," David said. "Buffalo skulls were sacred to the Lakota. The buffalo skull identifies them. So it must be part of their dance ceremony."

"Now, who do you think this strange-looking Indian with white-and-blue stripes on his red-painted face looking at us with a blank and hypnotic look is?" Michelle said, suddenly afraid. "The one wearing a huge Buffalo head with horns and feathers hanging on the side of it. Do you think he is a chief?"

"I think he is a medicine man," David said. "He has all kinds of paint on his face and weird stuff around his neck."

"Don't all Indians have painted faces?" Michelle asked, focusing on the man's white face.

"Not all the time," David said. "You think I know a lot, but I am not an encyclopedia with all the answers."

"Well, about the white paint?" Michelle asked persistently. "Do you know what the white paint means?"

"Hmmm," David said. "For the Native American, paint is critical. It represents different things. Certain colors identify the medicine man because he is important. He heals people, explains visions, and protects them from evil spirits. Let me think for a minute what white paint means."

"He looks like a ghost," Michelle said.

"I remember that white is very meaningful," David said. "It symbolizes the spirit of the world, which gives them strength."

"OK, is that your best answer? Because I knew that," Michelle said, vexed. She knew lots of stuff. David didn't have to explain *everything*.

"Then why did you ask?" David said.

"Just to make sure," Michelle said, looking all around her and trying to make sense of what was happening.

Pointing at a man wearing a very long headdress whose back was turned to them, David added, "I think he is the chief. He's wearing the long headdress."

"I know about headdresses," Michelle said, huffing. "I don't know though if his face is painted because I can't see it. But I do see he's holding a pipe in his hand."

"He must be a very, very important chief," David said. "His headdress has feathers going all the way to the ground."

"I knew that too," Michelle said.

David shook his head in frustration.

"And each feather represents an act of bravery," Michelle added confidently, proud of her knowledge. "So he is also very brave."

"Who do you think he is?" David asked. "If only we could see his face...I mean, what do you think his name is, since you always seem to know what I know?"

"You're the one who always has the answer," Michelle said. "So you tell me."

"How would I know?" David said, completely in the dark.

"There must be something about him we could identify," Michelle said. "How about the gold feathers? Maybe his name is Brave Gold Feather?"

"I don't think so," David said. "Since every chief wears feathers in his hair, it would mean every chief's name would be Brave Feather."

"Not necessarily so," Michelle said, feeling stupid. "Those feathers seem unique. I have never seen feathers like this."

"The feathers are from the golden eagle, one of the largest birds in North America," David said proudly. "And don't say you knew that too."

"I'm not going to say that because I didn't know," Michelle said. "Maybe we will see a golden eagle."

"I hope so," David said. "Wouldn't it be something?"

"By the way, I thought Mrs. Savant said a chief could also be a medicine man," Michelle said.

"He could be both," David said. "Remember she also said each tribe could have several chiefs and medicine men, and there were many subtribes with their own leaders, but they all came together and worked together in times of trouble."

"Why do you think the medicine man is looking at us so seriously?" Michelle asked.

After a few more minutes of observing the scene around her, Michelle asked, "Are the Indians going to hurt us because we look different and are not Indians?"

"We are only children," David answered. "Indians only killed when they were *provoked.* They wanted to live freely on their land, and white people would not let them. We, as children, are not threatening them."

"Not all Indians were good," Michelle said. "Some were very mean."

"There are bad people everywhere," David said.

"His blank look is spooky," Michelle remarked. "I feel he is looking through us."

"Maybe he is," David acknowledged. "Don't you think he is as surprised to see us as we are to be here? He must think we are a vision, the answer to their dance."

"Maybe he thinks we are spirits from another world," Michelle said.

3

What Are You Doing in the Dance Circle?

"What are you guys doing in the circle of dancers?" a boy their age asked, dragging both David and Michelle out of the circle.

Michelle stared at this cute black-haired boy with braids held by a multicolored weaved bandana, high cheekbones, and huge black eyes. He was wearing a red vest with a picture of two chiefs with long headdresses riding a white-and-brown horse.

The color of his vest matches my shoes, Michelle thought.

"It's not polite to stare," David whispered to Michelle.

"I can't help it," she whispered back. "He is so cute with his clothes and bow and arrows."

"You have seen many pictures of Indians before," David murmured.

"This is different," Michelle said. "This is the real thing."

"It's rude," David said. "How would you like it if someone did that to you?"

"The medicine man did," Michelle answered.

"Exactly my point," David said. "And you didn't feel good about it."

Michelle shrugged her shoulders and said, "You're right, but I'm not done looking at him. I promise I will stop in a minute."

"Who are you?" asked the boy with a bow and arrow hanging on his shoulder and a necklace of porcupine quills around his neck. "Where did you come from?"

Interesting necklace! Michelle thought. *Would I ever wear something like this? Hmm.*

"David and this is my friend Michelle," David answered the first question and ignored the second.

"I am Washta," said the handsome boy, wearing buckskin pants and moccasins.

What great-looking moccasins! Michelle thought, admiring the wolves and eagles decorating the moccasins.

"Washta," David said. "Is this a common name?"

"What does *Washta* mean?" asked Michelle, still mesmerized by the handsome black-haired boy who looked so different from anyone she had ever met.

"Washta means 'good,'" he answered. "This is my first name. I will get another name when I am older, after I accomplish a meaningful act."

"That's a nice name," Michelle said.

"Why will you get to get another name?" David asked. "Isn't Washta a good enough name?"

"There is a tradition with the Lakota," Washta answered. "A baby gets his name from something meaningful that has happened to his father, and then, when that baby gets older, he gets another name from something he himself has done or a vision he has had."

"So what happened to your father?" David asked.

"Me...I am an exception. My father thought I was the quietest baby ever to be born," Washta said. "He thought the name fit me perfectly. It was different for me; I didn't get my name for an act of bravery my father accomplished."

David and Michelle looked at each other and shrugged. They had thought there would be an incredible story attached to the name *Washta* and were kind of disappointed there was not, even though they thought it was a good name. They also thought it was nice that his father had felt that Washta was his most important achievement.

"What were you two doing dancing the grass dance?" he asked, surprised.

David wasn't sure how to answer. He couldn't tell Washta he had wished on a magic coin. So again, he didn't answer.

At that moment, a boy who looked like Washta but was a little taller and older passed right by them holding five hoops.

The dancers slowed their dances to let the older boy holding the hoops in. The boy passed by the dancing Indians and went to the center of the human circle. He put all his hoops on the ground except one.

"This is my brother Kohona," Washta said proudly. "He is different than us. He doesn't like hunting or running. He prefers to be alone, watching the movement of eagles, bears, snakes, and birds, and then he imitates their movements using his hoops. Have you ever seen a hoop dance?"

"No," David answered. "Is that an important dance?"

"All dances are important. The hoop dance is a happy dance," Washta said. "We dance to celebrate life by thanking the Great Spirit for Mother Earth and what she gives us—the plants, the animals, the water, the air we breathe..."

"Why did you stop us from dancing then?" Michelle asked. "Shouldn't we celebrate life too?"

"Ah, ha, ha!" Washta laughed. "Of course, everyone should. But, you see, my brother is going to do the hoop dance, and he needs space. I was trying to help you out before people got upset and asked you questions like what you were doing there."

Kohona twirled the hoop, moving around the circle of people.

"I didn't know the hoop was that important," Michelle said, surprised.

"The hoop has no beginning and no ending," Washta explained. "It represents the never-ending circle of life. The hoop also represents unity."

"Interesting. I never thought of the circle like that," Michelle said. "You know, I can dance with a hoop." She bent down to pick one up but was stopped immediately by the medicine man, who shook his fingers at her, indicating she should not do that.

Michelle blushed. She looked at David, who smiled at her, thinking nothing of her act. They both stood there, attentively watching Kohona.

Kohona continued with the one hoop slithering like a snake. He picked up the second hoop and put them together in front of him, opening them like a mouth.

"He is mimicking a snake," Michelle said, pleased she had figured out what Kohona was doing.

"Yes," Washta said, proud of his brother.

"How did you figure this out?" David asked, impressed. "Pretty good, Michelle."

Michelle smiled.

"Is the snake opening its mouth?" she asked, fascinated by all of Kohona's moves.

"It looks like it," David said, sure of himself.

Then Kohona picked up two more hoops, rolled all the hoops in the air, and lined them up behind his back, forming wings, which he flapped.

"He is a butterfly," said Michelle, clapping.

"Yeah," Washta said.

"You did it again," David said. "Bravo!"

Kohona continued rolling the hoops on the ground and above and all around him. He hopped like a rabbit and spun like an eagle in flight. He mimed the movement of other birds as well.

"Your brother is fantastic with mimicking the movement of different birds even though I can't tell what birds they are," Michelle said. "I can only do one thing, and it is to swirl around with one hoop."

"Can you do what your brother does with the hoops?" David asked Washta.

"No," Washta said. "It is unique to my brother."

Then, little by little, the drums got louder, and the women, dressed in long buckskin dresses, and the men, wearing breechclouts with leggings and buckskin shirts, started chanting and dancing. All were wearing beautiful moccasins. Some were stomping their feet, and others were swaying like grass in the field while moving in a circle. In a few minutes, Kohona's hoop dance was finished. He was done, so he left with the hoops in the direction of a tepee.

"Look! There are hoops over there by the stretched buffalo skin on sticks," David said, unsure they should move from where they were.

"Great idea, David," Michelle said, wanting to show Washta how good she was with the hoop.

"Let's go look at them. Come with me," Washta said and walked toward the hoops under the watchful eyes of the somber medicine man, who was now taking green herbs out of a medicine bag decorated with shells and sprinkling some in every direction—east, west, north, and south.

Michelle and David, keeping their eyes on the strange medicine man, followed Washta to the hoops.

"Look! The medicine man is taking some green herbs out of his bag," Michelle told David.

"He is praying," Washta said as the medicine man continued sprinkling the herbs in every direction.

"He is sprinkling the green herbs up, down, left, and right," Michelle said.

"Yes, he is calling every part of the universe to join in his prayer," Washta said. "East, west, north, and south."

4

The Medicine Man's Strange Ways and Looks

"Is he putting a curse on us?" Michelle asked as they walked by the medicine man.

"Of course not," Washta said. "Why would he? He is a good medicine man. He does good things for people. He is asking the Great Spirit to bless everyone with happiness."

Washta picked one of the hoops and handed one to Michelle. She quickly slid it over her head to her waist and started swinging the hoop.

"You are very good!" Washta exclaimed. "Maybe you should join my brother for the next dance."

The medicine man was watching the children, who looked different from the ones of his village, attentively, but he felt all children were nevertheless gifts from the Creator and should be treated in high esteem.

"Why is the medicine man still looking at me?" Michelle asked, nervous.

"He is not looking at you," Washta said. "He is praying. That's the way he looks when he is praying. He is a trusted man, advisor, and healer. He takes care of people."

"Look! I think the medicine man is calling you... *us*," David said, observing the medicine man with his arms motioning them to move closer to him.

"He is," Washta said, surprised to see the medicine man waving his hands and calling them. "Let's go see him. I'm sure it won't take long. We will be right back to play with the hoops."

"Is it because I touched the hoop when Kohona was doing his dance and I wasn't supposed to?" Michelle asked, uncomfortable and afraid to see the medicine man up close.

"I don't think so," Washta replied. "He must think you are a vision come alive, just like I did when I saw you."

"I'm scared," Michelle whispered in David's ear.

"Don't be," David said, sure of himself. He had the coin and would use it to go back home if he thought something bad was going to happen. "Everything is going to be OK."

They walked expectantly toward the Indian man with the white-striped face and many objects hanging around his neck.

"Look! He has a necklace with teeth around his neck," Michelle said. "I find that scary, don't you?"

"Yep, a bit strange," David said. "But those teeth are not human but animal. His necklace has pearls and different colored stones too. Those are not scary."

"OK, but still there are a lot of other bizarre things on the necklace," Michelle said. "You can't even tell what those things are; it's so weird."

"He is a medicine man after all," David said.

Washta's mom, Wise Owl, appeared suddenly. "I see the medicine man has called you to approach him."

"He did," Washta said respectfully and politely.

"You know it's an honor," the beautiful dark-haired woman said.

"I know," Washta replied softly but proudly.

"He even has a whistle," Michelle said. "Now why does he have a whistle?"

"What is it made of?" David asked.

"The whistle is made of a golden eagle wing bone," Washta answered. "Most of the time, the whistle is carried for protection, though the medicine man might have other reasons to carry one."

"Does he always have a pouch with him?" Michelle asked.

"Yes," Washta said. "His pouch is filled with herbs and holds a sacred round stone, *Tunka*, named for the god of rocks. There are four hundred and five sacred stones kept in gourds used for the Yuwipi ceremony."

"What's so special about the sacred stone?" Michelle asked.

"It has special power," Washta said. "All the stones have a hidden message, and the medicine man is able to communicate with them and hear their message. There is a story behind the Yuwipi ceremony."

"What is a Yuwipi ceremony?" David asked.

"Tell us," Michelle said. "I want to know."

Washta stopped a few feet from the chanting medicine man, indecisive about what to do—tell the story now or wait until later.

"The medicine man is waiting for us. I don't have time to explain the ceremony nor tell you the story. Maybe later," Washta said. "All I will tell you right now is this; when the White Buffalo Calf Woman gave us the sacred pipe, she also gave us a little red rock made of the lifeblood of our people. On it were seven circles, seven ways to worship with the pipe. When someone needs help, the pipe is often used along with the gourds and the sacred stones—"

"Washta, come closer," the medicine man interrupted, shaking a short branch and a shield with rattles and bells. He resumed his chanting.

"David, I told you the medicine man has some strange objects," Michelle told David in a soft voice. "Look at the snake circling the branch he is shaking. There is a transparent stone with feathers in its mouth."

"It's quartz," David said. "I read about this stone the Lakota medicine men have."

Washta approached the medicine man without hesitation. David followed more cautiously while Michelle dragged slowly in the back.

"Medicine Man, here we are," Washta said energetically.

The medicine man continued chanting rhythmically, keeping his eyes closed and brandishing his stick and his shield in all directions.

"Why is he shaking a shield while looking at us?" Michelle asked.

"It's a mandala," Washta said. "It brings luck to the person carrying it."

"I'd like to have one," Michelle whispered to David. "We might need luck while we're here."

All three were facing the odd medicine man.

"I'm scared," Michelle whispered quietly to David.

"Pretend we're at a costume party," David whispered back.

"OK, but this is a weird costume party," Michelle conceded.

~

Then the medicine man opened his eyes and talked to Washta in the Lakota language.

Washta nodded, placed himself between David and Michelle, and took their hands. He held their hands, and they formed a circle with the medicine man.

The chanting medicine man took his stick and danced it over the head of each of the children while sprinkling some herbs all around them.

David and Michelle watched the medicine man in awe, not knowing what to expect next. Would they be transformed into an animal?

Mrs. Savant had talked about the Indians but never said much about the medicine men.

Then the medicine man approached David, took some herbs, and rubbed some behind one of his ears while chanting. He repeated the same act on Washta and Michelle.

Michelle and David looked at each other.

"I still feel the same," Michelle said in a very soft voice. "Nothing has happened to us."

"But nothing is supposed to happen to you," Washta said in low voice and laughed. He didn't want to upset or disrupt the serious medicine man, who was now looking at the sky.

The children followed his look.

"David, look at the majestic hawk flying above your head!" Michelle shouted, ecstatic. "The medicine man must have called it. Otherwise, why would there be a hawk at this very moment."

A splendid red-tailed hawk was flying above them. The medicine man suddenly became agitated and closed his eyes.

"Why is the hawk still flying over us?" David asked Washta. "Is this good or bad?"

"A hawk is a very good sign," Washta said.

Finally the medicine man opened his eyes and said wisely, "Children, the hawk is bringing a message."

The medicine man paused and studied the hawk circling above, flying higher and higher gracefully and effortlessly.

"The hawk will protect all three of you by giving you wisdom in the choices you make," the medicine man said calmly. "You now may go."

"Do you think we will see buffalo?" Washta asked the medicine man.

"You will see much," the medicine man answered. "Use your common sense to guide you wisely."

The hawk had disappeared.

"Let's go do some more hoop dancing," David said, joking.

"Great idea," Washta said.

5

Washta's Unusual Puppies

Washta, David, and Michelle went back to the hoops.

This time, only David used a hoop and Michelle and Washta watched.

David picked up a hoop and tried to twirl it around his waist, but it kept falling down. He couldn't get the hang of it. And then, *bang*, something hit him on the back of the legs.

"Well, hello there, little puppy," David said and laughed. "Are you trying to show me how to use the hoop?"

The puppy, whitish-gray with red mixed in, kept jumping on David.

"Taka, take it easy. Come here," Washta called, and the puppy obediently left David. "Taka loves to play. He is protecting me. He doesn't know who you are. He is making his presence known."

The little puppy stopped at Michelle for a few seconds and then ran to Washta.

"Protecting you? Isn't he just a puppy?" Michelle said, petting the friendly puppy. "How old is he?"

"Taka is only two months old," Washta answered. "I found him and his brother all by themselves in a rock crevice with the mom lying next to them a few weeks ago. She must have been sick. The dad was nowhere to be found. I am not sure what happened. He would not have left them alone purposely, so something bad must have happened to him too. Wolves are very devoted to their families, but without their mom, they needed help surviving. So I became their family. They adopted me and I them. Even at a few months old, the wolves are protective."

"It's a wolf!" Michelle exclaimed in shock. "Wow! A wolf! Aren't wolves dangerous?"

"They can be, but these are not," Washta said, embracing his pet wolf. "They are tame. I have been taking care of them since they were babies. I will release them in the woods in a few weeks."

"I love its white fur," Michelle said, still petting the friendly wolf puppy.

David had given up on the hoop dance and approached Taka.

"Good dog," he said, letting him smell his hand. "Does he get lonely without his parents?"

"No, he has lots of attention from everyone," Washta said. "And he has his brother Itko."

"Where is Itko?" David asked.

"Taka, where is Itko?" Washta asked, looking deep into Taka's eyes. "Is Itko up to something again?" He added, "Itko has a mind of his own; he is always getting into trouble. He's the opposite of Taka, who is always good."

Taka wagged his tail and looked at Washta.

"Itko! Itko!" called Washta.

Itko didn't respond. Washta was a little concerned, even though Itko always came back. He still worried something might happen to him.

~

Washta saw the chanting medicine man still shaking seeds in all directions and looking at the sky.

Washta looked at the sky and saw the majestic golden-brown hawk now circling above a hill behind the village.

"I'm not sure why this hawk is circling above," Washta said. "Maybe it's trying to tell me something. Maybe it's about Itko. Let's go find Itko."

Washta started running in the direction of the hills, passing an impressive tepee painted with various animals and Indians in action when a hand suddenly grabbed him.

"Where are you going in a hurry?" asked a soft voice.

"Mother!" Washta said, surprised to see his mother had stopped him.

"Well?" Wise Owl, Washta's mom, asked.

"I saw a hawk flying above the hill. It's calling me," Washta said. "Itko is missing. The hawk knows where he is."

"I'm sure he does," Wise Owl answered. "I saw your little friends earlier in the dance circle. Before you go searching, I would like to make your friends feel welcome in our midst by giving them a gift," she said, holding out a pretty little buckskin dress and a pair of buckskin leggings.

Washta stopped. He didn't want to be disrespectful to his mom, even though he was dying to run up the hill in search of Itko. He wanted to be there before the hawk disappeared.

Michelle approached Wise Owl and said, "Hi, Wise Owl. I am Michelle. I love your dress."

"Thank you, Michelle. Welcome to our village," Wise owl said. "I just finished making a little girl's dress and a pair of leggings. Both have fringes. You are the same size as my daughter. Will you accept the dress?"

"Of course. It's beautiful," Michelle said, slipping the dress on. "I always wanted to look like an Indian princess and wear a dress like this."

"You do look like a princess," Wise Owl said and grinned. "You look like you belong here."

"It fits perfect, and it's so soft," Michelle added, adjusting the dress, which was stuck on her hips because of her clothes underneath the dress.

"It's buckskin," said the proud Indian woman.

"You look like a Native American," David said.

"Your turn to try on some clothes," Michelle said.

Wise Owl looked at David and said, "I have the perfect clothes for you. How about these leggings? You and Washta will look like twins."

She handed the animal leggings to David, who quickly slipped them on.

"You look weird with your shirt," Michelle said and laughed. "Take it off, and you will look like Washta."

"No, I will not take my shirt off," David replied. "My skin is too white. I'll look like a ghost. The medicine man is really going to be spooked and dunk me in a tub of his special herbs to make my skin darker."

Michelle laughed so hard she couldn't stop. So did Washta.

Wise Owl said, "I have an idea." There was a pile of clothes in front of her. She bent down, picked up a vest, and handed it up to David.

"I just finished this vest," she said. "This is exactly what you need."

David put on the vest.

"Wise Owl is right," Michelle said, agreeing. "Now you have the right look."

"Thank you, Wise Owl," David said.

Michelle took her wampum necklace off and offered it to Wise Owl.

"Wise Owl, thank you again for the beautiful dress," Michelle said. Holding out her necklace of shells, she said, "Wise Owl, this is for you," offering the woman the beautiful wampum necklace she had worked so long and hard to make.

Wise Owl was surprised to receive a gift from a little girl.

"*Philamayaye*," Wise Owl said with tears in her eyes, putting the necklace around her neck.

6

Michelle Throws a Stick at the Medicine Man

Taka started barking and ran in the direction of the hill.

"Go after Taka," Wise Owl said. "But please be careful."

"Let's go, David," Washta said, running.

David followed with Michelle even though Washta had not invited her.

"Look at all the buffalo skins on the ground," Michelle remarked as they were passing women bent over the skins, scraping them.

"It looks like strenuous work," David answered. "Did you see how intensely the women are scrubbing the skins?"

"Indian women work very hard," Michelle said, looking at all the women busy doing things she thought a man should have been doing.

David was in awe, watching one woman removing something from a buffalo that resembled a brain. He was so stunned he didn't watch where he was going and tripped over one of the stakes holding a buffalo skin and plunged forward into a stretched skin hanging on upright posts.

"Is that what I think it is?" David asked, overwhelmed, as he was getting back to his feet. "Is she pulling out a brain off the head of a bison?"

"Yuck! Disgusting!" Michelle uttered, covering her eyes with her hand. "You mean buffalo?" she added.

"Yes," David said. "I said bison because that's the right name. The word buffalo came about because the first explorers, the French, called the bison *boeuf,* and the English, who came later, kept saying *buffle,* which became buffalo."

"I knew that," Michelle said, reopening her eyes.

Washta stopped running and came back to stand by David and Michelle to explain. "Yes, she is. Once the buffalo are brought here, women take over," Washta said. "They use every part of the buffalo. They skin, cut, and cook the animal. The brain, for example, will be mashed and rubbed on the hide. Not one piece of the buffalo is wasted. Doesn't your mother skin buffalo?"

"No, I don't think my mom has ever seen a buffalo," David said. "But she does skin chicken once in a blue moon."

"Chicken?" Washta asked. "I have eaten turkey, but not chicken. Is it good?"

"Yes, very good," David answered. "I think it is better than turkey."

"I prefer buffalo stew," Washta said. "My mother makes the best one. She is making some now. We'll try it later with corn bread. Wouldn't you like to?"

"Yes," David replied quickly. He couldn't wait to see what buffalo meat was all about.

Michelle didn't say anything about the stew. She didn't want to eat buffalo meat; she wasn't hungry. But she nevertheless was curious about why they would use the brain.

"Why do they use the brain and not some other buffalo part?" Michelle asked.

"What's so special about the brain?" David, also curious, asked.

"The brain has lots of fat and water," Washta said. "We spread the brain fat on the buffalo skin. That's what makes buffalo skin bend easily, and it also makes it waterproof."

"Interesting," David said.

"Yes, it is," Michelle said, looking around.

Michelle had heard enough about the brain. To hear more would make her sick.

She saw some kids their age playing and became more interested in the different games they played.

Some were playing with hoops, and others with buffalo heads on their heads were running toward each other, trying to capture one another.

"What are these boys doing?" Michelle asked, pointing at two teenagers with spears and a small ring.

Washta and David looked at the boys with the spears.

"This is one of our favorite games," Washta said. "The game trains our eyes and hand for accuracy. David, do you want to try?"

"How about me?" Michelle asked.

"Sure, you can play too," Washta said and laughed. "If you want to go barefoot and naked."

Michelle thought for a minute and said unshyly, "No problem. You and David go first, and then it will be my turn."

"David, take your shoes and shirt off," Washta said.

She watched the two boys take their footwear and shirts off.

"I knew you wouldn't go naked," Michelle said scornfully.

"We are almost naked," David said.

Washta went to the two boys who had just finished their run and asked to borrow their spears and the small ring wrapped in buffalo sinew.

"Here is the spear that we will run with," Washta said, giving the spear to David. He looked at Michelle and said, "Michelle, do you think you could handle running with a five-foot spear?"

"Why not?" Michelle answered with her nose up. "Because I'm a girl you think I can't? I can do anything you guys do."

"Hmmm," Washta said, not believing her. "Anyway, watch what we do with the spear. I'll throw the ring, and both David and I will run very fast after the ring rolling along. The goal is for both of us to hit the rolling ring so that our spears cross each other through the ring at the same time."

"Easy," Michelle said, defiantly crossing her arms. She thought, *That does sound impossible to do, putting the spear inside the ring at the same time. I want to see David do that.*

David laughed. He knew Michelle was always up for a challenge. Most of all though, she hated being told she could not do what a boy could do. That fired her up.

She started watching other games being played while keeping an eye on Washta and David's game. Soon, she was tired of doing nothing. She was getting antsy and wanted to play at one of the games. She decided to play a game. But which game? *Which one looks the most interesting?*

A little round object rolled to her feet and distracted her, taking her attention away from David and Washta's game.

She picked the little ball up. *It looks like a marble, but it isn't,* she thought. As she examined it, she realized it was the tip of a buffalo horn. A little girl had thrown it at her feet and was soon there to collect it. She immediately went back to her friends, who were playing with the marbles, sliding them into a hole made in the hard soil.

She saw some kids holding two sticks, one long and one short. They put the short stick over a hole and the long stick under it; then they lifted the short one quickly into the air, trying to make it fly as far as they could. With the long stick, each would measure how many sticks away the short stick was lying from the hole. The winner was the one who had thrown the stick the farthest away.

Then, Michelle saw two sticks on the ground. *That's the game I'm going to play*.

She stooped and picked them up. She put the short one over the hole like she had seen some kids do, and with the longer stick, she lifted the short one off the ground, sending it flying through the air directly in front of her. She hit the medicine man's leg. He immediately turned around with a scary look on his face; he dropped his sacred shield decorated with rattles.

"I'm sorry," Michelle said, blushing and looking at the ground, afraid to look into the medicine man's chilling eyes. "I didn't mean to hit you. I didn't see you."

David had seen the whole thing, and he ran back to Michelle. So did Washta.

"Uh-oh, he dropped his mandala or sacred shield," David said. He had just finished playing with the spear.

The medicine man mumbled something. He was now perturbed. He had let go of his sacred shield. He quickly picked up the sacred drum and raised his eyes to the sky, chanting, wailing, and dancing frenetically in a circle, as if begging for forgiveness.

Washta came to Michelle. "It's going to be OK, as long as no one touched the sacred skin covering the shield. Now he is dancing and playing the drum, hoping to recapture the close union he had with the soul of Mother Earth. He probably thinks he hurt Mother Earth's feeling and lost her favor. He wants to communicate with the earth mother because, you see, he now thinks he has lost her favor."

"Just because when the stick hit him he dropped the drum?" Michelle asked nervously. "I shook him out of his trance. He looks upset. Do you think he is mad at me? I am surprised to see him so close to us. We left him at the circle with the dancers. He popped up out of nowhere. I never saw him."

"At times, it feels as if he is everywhere," Washta said.

"Now that I hit him with a stick, he must think I am evil," Michelle said. "He probably wants to change me into a bird or something."

"I don't understand why you are so afraid of him. He doesn't do magic," Washta added. "He doesn't harm people; he helps them. He is very sensitive to people's needs. Believe me; he is praying for something good. That is what he does all the time."

"Michelle, why are you being such a scaredy-cat all of a sudden?" David asked his long-time friend.

"You never said anything about visiting a real Indian village," Michelle whispered in David's ear. "It's one thing to climb trees and play at home. But to be face to face with real Indians is—"

"Oh! Come on. It's not that bad," David said, interrupting her.

"Can we go back home please before something bad happens?" Michelle begged.

"In a little bit," David answered. "We just got here."

7

The Medicine Man Gives a Shield to David

As the medicine man was dancing around, holding his rattle and drum, a dragonfly came and perched on his shoulder.

Washta approached the medicine man slowly, as he didn't want to disturb the praying man or the dragonfly. The medicine man was oblivious to everything around him and continued his dance. The dragonfly left the medicine man and went to Washta and then to David.

The medicine man opened his eyes and saw the dragonfly on David. He came to David and danced around him, mumbling a happy chant.

"What is the medicine man saying?" David asked.

"The medicine man said Mother Earth is blessing you," Washta listened and replied. "You are to be a messenger."

"A messenger?"

"Yes," Washta answered.

"Hmm...a messenger?" Michelle said, puzzled. "What do you think the message will be?"

"I think you will tell of your time here." Washta thought for a minute and then said seriously, "It will be a message of truth about our people."

The medicine man then took a small shield and handed it to David, who examined it carefully before saying, "Thank you; it's beautiful."

"It is beautiful," Michelle said, looking at the impressive round red shield with its four feathers. "I love the falcon drawing and the feathers."

"Isn't the falcon a great observer of everything around it?" David asked.

"Yes, it's very meaningful," Washta said. "And the shield will bring you luck."

The medicine man, still chanting, left them and went into a tepee.

"Please, Michelle, no more games," David advised her.

"I know," Michelle said, contrite. "But I hit him by accident. He popped up from nowhere."

Taka, who had followed very quietly, started jumping on David. The dragonfly flew away.

"Taka, let's go find Itko," Washta said. "I think I know where he is. Follow me."

8

The Magical Tree

They resumed their walk.

David and Michelle followed Washta and Taka. Taka knew where Washta was going. Every day, Washta would go to the top of the small hill to survey and scout the plains below. He was on the lookout for buffalo, which were becoming rarer.

Michelle was happy to leave the strange-looking Indian medicine man behind.

"Look at the white weasel by the tree in front of us," David said.

"How beautiful is that!" Michelle said. She couldn't wait to see it up close. "It's the first time I have seen a weasel."

"The weasel is always around," Washta said. "You will see many other animals." He added, "We, Lakota value all wildlife and respect their way of life. The weasel is cute, but it is a wild animal, and we know to let it alone."

Michelle didn't listen. She couldn't help herself. She ran toward the cuddly white weasel, following Taka, who had seen the weasel first.

"The weasel can bite, so don't go too close," Washta warned.

But the weasel ran away, quick to disappear in the many bushes and trees surrounding them.

"I guess the weasel wants to be left alone," David said.

"Where did it go?" Michelle asked, running and moving the branches out of her way. "The grass is high around here. There are too many bushes around. It's impossible to keep track of anything, even if it is moving."

"But look what has just showed up behind the tree." Washta said, pointing to a pretty fox. "There is a red fox. Have you ever seen a red fox?"

"No," David and Michelle answered in unison.

"Where is it?" David asked.

Taka had seen the red fox and ran after it, forgetting about the weasel.

So did Michelle, reluctantly giving up on the weasel for a moment.

"Do you see the red fox?" Michelle asked. "I don't."

Not seeing the red fox, she went back to looking furiously for the weasel but soon gave up for good. "I lost sight of the weasel so it doesn't matter anymore; I might as well look for a red fox."

All three pursued Taka, who was now on a mission to get the red fox. David and Michelle were very curious to see a red fox.

"I don't see the red fox," David said.

"Let's follow Taka," Washta suggested. "He gave up on the weasel the minute he saw the fox."

They eagerly followed Taka and Washta.

࿐

All of a sudden, Taka stopped at a tall green elm tree and barked furiously. Had he really forgotten the white weasel, which had disappeared? Why was he barking at the tree?

"This tree is special," Washta said, stopping a few feet from the tree to get a wider view. "It is on sacred ground, and when we get near, look closely, pay attention, and you will see all kinds of living things on and around the tree and all around us."

"What kinds of things?" David asked.

"Animals," Washta said. "Insects, but mostly animals."

"How about elves?" Michelle asked.

"Michelle, there are no elves here," David answered. "This is reality."

"Too bad," Michelle said and laughed.

"Let's get closer to the tree," David said.

David couldn't wait to get to this peculiar tree and see all those living things.

Taka was barking nonstop at the tree.

"OK, no elves, but I don't see the fox either," Michelle said, stopping halfway to the tree and looking all around for something unusual. "But where could the weasel have gone?"

"Oh! Forget about the weasel," David said softly.

"OK," Michelle conceded. "But it would have been nice to see it up close."

"Do you think Taka is barking at the weasel or the fox?" David asked.

"I'm not sure," Washta answered, examining the tree.

"Where did the red fox go?" David asked.

"Believe me; he is around," Washta said. "Even though the little red fox is fast, he is always looking for something to eat."

"He is probably after the weasel," Michelle said.

"Maybe," Washta said.

"Could it eat a weasel?" she asked.

"It could," Washta answered. "But it prefers crickets, grasshoppers, beetles, birds, and rabbits. *Itko*, where are you?" he called out.

But Itko didn't answer.

9

The Cat with No Tail

There was a meow-growl close by and then another. A series of more howls, grunts, whines, and wails followed.

"There is a cat in the tree," Michelle said. "I hear it meowing."

"You're right. Taka must have heard the cat too," David said, searching the tree with his eyes but seeing nothing. "Where is it?"

"Are you sure it's a cat?" Washta said in a teasing way, knowing it was not an ordinary cat who hung around the elm.

"I bet Taka knows for sure," David said.

"Let's go find out," Washta answered.

All three ran to Taka, who was waiting by the elm. They stood by Taka, looking at a spotted kitten now sitting quietly on a branch of the densely foliated tree filled with chirping birds.

"What is Taka looking at?" Michelle asked. "I can't see the cat. All I see are leaves."

"Keep looking," Washta said gently. "It's there."

"I see it," David said.

The spotted kitten, hearing noise below, started climbing up and retreated quickly higher, safely out of sight up the revered elm. Taka saw the cat move up. He couldn't stand still. He wanted to play with the small cat, which was high up in the tree. Powerless to get to the cat, he circled the tree, barking and barking—to no avail. The wise cat had no interest in a noisy dog. It ignored all the brouhaha below and continued playing with leaves as it climbed higher.

"Oh! Look! Look! Now I see what Taka is looking at." Michelle shrieked with delight, pointing to the small animal in the tree. "A cute little kitten. What do you think happened to its tail?"

"Silly, it was born that way," David said. "Don't you know what it is?"

"No," Michelle said. "I'm not as good as you at identifying the animals and knowing all their names."

"It's a wildcat," David explained. "It's a bobcat."

"A bobcat!" Michelle said, surprised. "Aren't they dangerous?"

"No," David answered. "They're very shy. They are dangerous to small animals, but we are too big for them."

"This is quite an adventure you dragged me into," Michelle said, amused. "Indians, wolves, and now a bobcat."

"Stick with me, and you will never be bored," David said.

"Oh, I know that," Michelle said. "You're always fun. By the way, how do you know it is a bobcat and not just a plain old cat who lost its tail?"

Taka seemed fascinated by the sight of this little brownish cat with pointed black ears and a white patch in the center. It stood on a branch, and he just stood there, looking at it but not barking.

"Because of the short tail, the ears, and the spotted, freckled coat it has," David answered. "Don't you think it looks a little bit like a tiger?"

"Hmm, kind of," Michelle concurred.

"We have more company," Washta said, pointing at the sky.

David and Michelle looked up at the sky.

"Washta, do you think the eagle wants the bobcat?" Michelle asked as the eagle circled above.

"There are all kinds of things happening around this tree—a fox, a bobcat, and a hawk or eagle..." Washta said. "That's why I called it the magic tree."

"Do you think the eagle is watching over us?" David asked, remembering what the medicine man had said.

"Maybe the eagle is interested in the bobcat," Washta said. "It's flying away now. I think it has something else in mind."

"You're right, Washta," Michelle said. "There are all kinds of things happening around this tree. A weasel, a fox, a bobcat, and now an eagle...What else are we going to see?"

"And there's more," Washta said.

"Wow!" Michelle said.

"I can't wait to see what else pops up," David said excitedly.

They heard a series of continuous warbling sounds, mechanical-sounding *whirrs* and *chirps*, and *cheep* calls and then a *churee* whistle.

"Did you hear that sound?" David asked.

"Yep," Washta answered.

"What's making that whistling sound?" Michelle asked.

"There are swallows, martins, and sparrows hiding in this tree," Washta answered. "Let's be quiet and listen."

The whistle came again.

"I figured it out," Washta answered. "It's a meadowlark."

A yellow meadowlark, whose nest was right by the bobcat, showed its head and whistled loudly at the intruder. The whistle startled the bobcat, which lost its footing and fell to a branch near the ground.

"How can you tell it's a meadowlark?" David asked.

"It whistled a few times, and then it made a few gurgling warbles," Washta said. "That's how the meadowlarks talk."

"Oh no!" Michelle said, rushing to the kitten. "It fell."

"Don't worry!" Washta said. "It will be right back on its feet."

"The kitten is playing with a green buffalo treehopper," David said, pointing to the green insect shaped like a buffalo.

"I love the color of that insect," Michelle said. "Is the bobcat going to eat the hopper?"

David shrugged his shoulders in disbelief.

"He might...but probably not; bobcats are mostly carnivorous," Washta said. "To him, the bird is much more appetizing than an insect, just as the weasel would be more interested in a bird."

Michelle quietly broke a small branch and approached the bobcat slowly. The bobcat growled and then wailed softly. Because he was still a kitten, Michelle knew he would like to play.

She presented the branch and started teasing the bobcat, who enjoyed the game. With his paws, he delicately touched and twirled the branch to Michelle's delight. She dared picked up the gentle kitten to Washta's distress and concern.

"Careful, Michelle," he warned, petting Taka to keep him quiet and away from the bobcat while keeping a lookout for the kitten's mom.

David was observing both Michelle and Washta.

"Why did the bobcat stop playing?" Michelle asked.

"I saw something white moving," Washta said. "The kitten must have seen the same thing."

Michelle, holding the gentle kitten, looked in the same direction as the kitten and saw the squealing weasel emerging from a hole in a small tree right next to the elm.

"I see the weasel!" Michelle shrieked with joy.

"Look at that," David said. "It was hiding inside the tree right by us."

"Phewy, something smells bad," Michelle said, pinching her nose and turning around to see, right behind her, a big black skunk with white stripes waddling toward a lizard, who was busy eating a cricket.

"The skunk wants the lizard," Washta said.

The skunk turned around.

"The skunk changed its mind," Michelle said. "It doesn't want a lizard anymore."

"He is going toward the tree hollow," David said.

"It's going to see the weasel," Michelle said.

"I was wondering if the skunk was going to notice who had invaded its space," Washta said. "The weasel took over the skunk's home."

"This is going to be interesting," David said. "I hope we don't get sprayed."

The growling skunk approached the tree hollow, fluffing its fur, shaking its tail, and stamping its feet in protest. It wasn't happy. The teasing weasel kept popping its head in and out of the tree hollow, playing hide-and-seek with the skunk.

"The weasel is quite a comedian," Michelle said, laughing. She was still holding the now restless kitten.

"Let go of the bobcat, Michelle," David ordered.

"What if it wants to eat the weasel or the skunk or the lizard?" Michelle asked.

"Any of the three would be a treat to him," Washta said. "Let's see what happens when you put the kitten down."

"OK," Michelle said, putting the kitten on the ground. "I don't like putting the kitty at risk. I'm not sure about this."

The bobcat walked away from the skunk and the weasel.

"He is turned off by the bad odor," David said and laughed. "No action here."

"Good. He's not interested," Michelle said. "He's going the opposite way."

"Like you," David said. "You quickly lost interest in the weasel."

"Is he going to eat the lizard?" Michelle asked, watching the bobcat going toward the lizard, who seemed frozen in place.

"Or is he more interested in the squawking baby bird?" Washta asked as the bobcat darted toward the baby bird, who somehow ended up next to the lizard.

"Oh! No. It's a baby owl!" Michelle said nervously, watching the helpless baby bird. "First the kitten fell and now a baby bird. Come back, little kitten. You can't eat the baby bird."

They all ran to the little kitten.

The bobcat didn't listen and walked gingerly up to the owlet.

"Come on, little kitty," Michelle said, afraid the bobcat would eat the baby bird.

"The bobcat won't eat the owlet," Washta said, hoping he was right.

"How did you get down here?" Michelle asked the owlet as if it could talk to her.

"It must have fallen," Washta answered. "Just like the bobcat."

"But how?" Michelle asked. "Is it hurt?"

"It doesn't look like it's hurt," David said. "It's moving around."

"Why wasn't the mom watching it?" Michelle asked.

"Where is the mom?" David asked, looking up the tree.

"She's around," Washta said. "The mom can't watch the babies all the time. She helps her mate hunt every so often when the babies are old enough. And since they took over a squirrel's nest, my guess is that the squirrel sneaked in when they were away and tried to get its nest back, probably accidentally ousting the owlet."

"This is so sad," Michelle said. "How do you know it took over a squirrel's nest?"

"I come here every day," Washta said. "I have seen squirrels where the owls are. The squirrels disappeared a while back."

"I don't see the parents anywhere," David said.

"How is the baby going to make it without its mom or dad?" Michelle asked.

"The baby will be OK," Washta said. "This happens often, and the mom and dad always come back. They're never out for long, just long enough to get food."

"Can't we put it back?" Michelle asked.

"It's better to let nature take care of it," Washta replied. "We could harm it."

"Look! There is a bushy-tailed brown squirrel hurriedly going up a tree," David said as he watched the squirrel climb merrily.

"Do you think it's the same squirrel?" Michelle asked. "Do you think it could hurt other owlets, assuming there are more?"

"It could, but it won't," Washta said.

"Squirrels are afraid of owls," David said. "Like Washta said, it must have fallen coincidentally."

The busy squirrel scampered and skipped from branch to branch. It didn't stop where the owl's nest was but continued to a branch directly above the chirping meadowlark.

"I sometimes hear the squirrel whistle when it feels danger," Washta said. "Believe it or not, owls eat squirrels, so do bobcats, foxes, and hawks."

"The squirrel didn't stop at the owl's nest," Michelle said, relieved. "Poor squirrel, everything wants to eat it."

"Where is it going?" David asked.

"When the owls took over its nest, the squirrel found another home in an abandoned woodpecker hole even though sometimes it forgets and goes back to its old home," Washta said. "That's where it is heading."

"It looks as if there might be a family of squirrels in there," David said, looking at some commotion going on around the woodpecker's nest.

"Pretty smart, Mrs. Squirrel," Michelle said. "To have found another home and leave the owls alone."

No one noticed the mother owl come back. She perched high on the tree, watching the squirrel walk by the owls' home and enter the woodpecker hole. The secure owl ignored the sprinting squirrel's back-and-forth activities and swooped down to help her baby. The bobcat, surprised at seeing a big bird close to it, scampered away. It left the owlet, wanting no war with the big bird.

The kitten was more interested in playing than having a fight. The owlet was too young for him. It would be no fun to play with it.

Michelle picked up the kitten one more time and hugged it, saying, "You decided against playing with the baby owl, didn't you? I'm glad."

"What are you doing?" David asked. "You should leave the kitten on the tree this time."

"Why?" Michelle demanded defiantly. "Nothing happened before. It's just a playful kitten."

"The mom has to be around," Washta said. "She wouldn't like it."

"The mom could get very upset with you," David answered. "You know she is bound to be on her way back. The kitten has been alone a long time."

"David is right, Michelle," Washta said. "The mom could get very aggressive."

"Oh! OK," Michelle said, putting the kitten down. It quickly scuttled and vanished in the nearby bushes. "The kitty disappeared quickly. Probably after the weasel."

"Yep," Washta said.

"It doesn't smell anymore," Michelle said. "The skunk has left the weasel alone."

"Well, hopefully," David said.

"This is quite a tree," Michelle said. "It has so much action."

They walked into an open field.

10

Eating Strawberries with the Deer

"Are you guys hungry?" Washta asked as he picked up a few strawberries hidden in a patch of grass.

Michelle and David walked over to Washta and discovered a whole new world.

"Wow!" Michelle said, looking at a field of yellow flowers sprinkled with lavender and pink ones guarded by berry and fruit trees.

"Look at all the berries," Michelle said.

"This is a haven for animals!" David exclaimed.

"And for us too," Washta said. "We love berries."

They picked up very red strawberries and big blueberries and sat down in the peaceful small meadow tucked in a series of trees, unaware of all the animals hidden among the grass and plants.

"These are the best strawberries I have ever eaten," Michelle said, careful not to drool the red syrup down her beautiful Indian dress.

They were sitting quietly—even Taka, who, believe it or not, also loved strawberries—absorbing the surreal scenery in front of them.

"If you look closely, you will see deer, mink, and bears," Washta said.

"Really?" Michelle said. "What a treat it would be to see deer! But bears, no."

"Look ahead in front of you," David said softly. "Your wish will come true."

"I see it," Michelle said. "It's a spotted fawn jerking its neck; it's aware we're here."

"Look again," David said. "There are three white-tailed deer."

"Wow! What a sight!" Michelle said. "They are chasing one another in a circle. They're so graceful."

"They're playing tag," David said, laughing.

"Can we get close?" Michelle asked Washta.

"I'm not sure how close you will be able to get. They're usually pretty skittish, but go ahead," Washta answered. "See, it's a good thing you don't have the kitten. It would have scared them away. You would have had to look at them from right here."

Michelle got up, holding a handful of strawberries, and went to the fawn. She approached the little fawn very, very slowly, offering her strawberries so as not to alarm it.

The deer stopped moving when they saw Michelle approach. They stood with their white tails up, and the fawn looked around for its mother, but the mother wasn't around. After a few minutes, the fawn hesitantly and shyly approached Michelle. Not feeling danger, it accepted her fruit offering.

Michelle was so happy to be standing next to the little fawn, she wanted to cry out in her joy, but she knew if she did move, the fawn would get spooked and run away. She continued feeding it the strawberries very quietly.

She then saw a big deer appear in the tall grass—and then another one and another one.

Is one of them the mother? Michelle wondered.

They just stood behind a tree, gazing past her into the distance with their white tails up, as if sensing danger.

Michelle wanted to say, *You are OK; I mean you no harm.*

"Look! There is a red fox eating a yellow squash!" David shouted.

David's shout startled the fawn and the deer, who moved away swiftly and retreated farther into the woods.

"Why did you shout?" an incensed Michelle said. "You scared the fawn away from me."

"Don't you want to see the red fox we didn't see earlier?" David said.

"Yes, I do but..." Michelle agreed. "But I was enjoying being close to the fawn. When can we get this close to a fawn at home? They are so pretty and precious. You scared it away," Michelle said, disappointed.

"The red fox is just as cute," David said. "I bet you have never seen a red fox."

"You're right. I've never seen a red fox," Michelle said, looking at the busy little fox. "He is cute but so much smaller than I thought. I always thought foxes were huge. This one is the size of a cat."

"A big cat," David corrected Michelle.

Washta walked calmly toward the red fox, and as he came close, five little foxes came out of a burrow hidden in leaves.

"Guys, hurry up," Washta said. "Look what I found camouflaged in the leaves."

David and Michelle quickly went to where Washta was kneeling.

"Oh! They're so cute, but are they going to eat the fawn?" Michelle asked, always concerned about the babies.

"The fawn is too big for them," Washta said. "Besides, they are busy eating the many fruits around. Foxes love strawberries, apples, blackberries, corn, and grass."

"That's good. I am glad to hear that," Michelle said, trying to catch one of the baby foxes.

"Michelle, I know you want to pet one," Washta said nicely, "but it's better you don't."

David gave her a pleading look.

"OK," Michelle said reluctantly. "The mom is right there. I don't want to upset her."

"Where did Taka go?" David asked.

"He's around," Washta said, unconcerned. "It's a lot of excitement for him. He wants to run after everything he sees, but he never goes far from me. Sometimes his animal instincts take over and push him to leave my sight."

"I never thought an Indian village would be that fun to explore," Michelle said. "And there are so many animals around."

"And there are more," Washta said. "Look what's ahead."

"More deer?" David asked, looking at a brown animal with a cream belly and throat and very black, short, branched horns.

"Are these goats?" Michelle asked.

"They may look like goats, but they are not," Washta answered.

"These are deer then?" Michelle said, looking at the goat-deer-looking animal.

"They have the body of a deer, but they are not deer," Washta said. "They are pronghorn antelope."

"They don't look like antelope," David said.

"Do you know they run faster than horses?" Washta said.

"I'd like to see that," Michelle said. She knew all about horses.

"They are the fastest animal in North America," David said, remembering what his mom, the zoologist, had said about pronghorns.

"You might see them run," Washta said. "They also have extraordinary eyesight; they see everything, and that is why they panic easily and run for their life when they think there is a predator close by."

"What's happening?" Michelle asked. "The antelope are running wild."

"You're getting your wish," Washta said. "Look how fast they run."

"Incredible," David said. "Nothing is going to harm them. They will outrun anything coming after them, even Itko who is trying to."

"Itko! Itko, come over here!" Washta shouted. "We have been looking for you. Why did you scare the pronghorns?"

Itko obeyed and came running toward Washta, followed by Taka.

"Itko," Washta repeated in a subdued voice. "Why did you run into the herd of pronghorn?"

Itko with his guilty eyes stood quietly looking at Washta.

Itko had suddenly reappeared as if he had heard David's wish. He ran to the group of pronghorn antelope, and the panicked pronghorn ran for their lives.

"What about those animals with the big, curved horns grazing by the antelope? Are they big goats?" Michelle asked, pointing at the animals next to the antelope.

"Those are bighorn sheep," Washta said casually.

"The pronghorn and the sheep all seem to get along," David said.

Michelle looked down and saw big berries. She bent down, and as she was about to pick up a berry, she saw a big rat scurrying among the berries, wanting a berry too.

"Eeek!" Michelle screamed, running away from the bush. "There is a big rat in the berry bushes."

David and Washta came running to the place where Michelle had just seen the nefarious beast do its misdeed.

"It's a muskrat," Washta said, laughing. "Usually they eat corn. This one must be ravenous."

"I knew it was a rat," Michelle reasserted.

"It is a muskrat, not a rat," David said. "It is much bigger than a rat but just as bad. It's a walking disease monster."

"A rat is a rat no matter how you look at it," Michelle affirmed. "It's bad and ugly."

"It's more like a beaver," Washta said.

"Is there water close by?" David asked. "Don't they usually live by water?"

"Yes," Washta answered. "There is a lot of water around here. The beavers and the muskrats are great friends and live together peacefully. I'll show you later."

"Interesting smell!" Michelle said from a distance, breathing in the musky odor. "What's that smell?"

"The muskrat sprays around his territory," Washta said.

"No comparison to the foul-smelling skunk spray," David said. "Michelle is right. They do look like big river rats but with long opossum-like tails, don't they?"

"Are they dangerous?" Michelle asked as she advanced cautiously toward the muskrat.

"No," Washta said. "They are peaceful animals."

At that moment, a handsome chocolate-brown mink appeared chasing a rabbit.

"Cute weasel," Michelle said, sure it was a weasel.

"You have a lot to learn about animals," David said. "It's not a weasel."

"This is a hungry mink," Washta said, running after the mink. "They have very soft fur. Have you ever touched a mink?"

"Not a live one," Michelle said.

"What do you mean 'not a live one'?" Washta asked, getting closer to the mink. "You touched a dead one?"

"My mom has a mink coat," Michelle answered. "And I love touching it."

"Washta, are you trying to catch it?" David asked, running right behind. "Wait for us."

"No," Washta said. "I'm just curious about where it's going."

At that moment, a muskrat peeked its head out of its house in the roots of a tree.

"Look what's checking out things!" Washta said.

"Another muskrat," David said, finally able to recognize one of the Dakotas' animals. "Mink love muskrats, don't they?"

"Yep," Washta responded.

"That's where the mink is going," Michelle said. "It wants a muskrat. Good riddance!"

The mink gave up on the rabbit and darted toward the muskrat, its favorite food.

Washta, however, arrived at the tree first, forcing the disconcerted mink to change its route and climb up the tree.

"Come here, mink!" David shouted, bumping into Washta.

In its panic, the mink jumped to the next tree and disappeared in its dense foliage.

"Bummer," Michelle said. "I would have loved to feel a live mink's fur."

"Why would it be different than your mom's coat?" David asked.

"Actually, I don't think you would have been able to get that close," Washta said, moving toward the tree where the mink had vanished.

The mink didn't see the hawk flying over the tree, watching everything around it. The hawk let out a screech, "Kee-eeee-ar," startling the mink. It lost its balance and fell on top of Washta's head.

"Ouch!" screamed Washta.

"Hahaha!" Michelle and David laughed.

"Nice hat!" Michelle said.

"It can't hurt," David said. "It's so tiny."

The agitated mink quickly jumped off Washta's head and went away, chasing yet another muskrat.

"That mink moves fast," Michelle said.

⁂

"Where to now?" David asked.

"We are almost at the lookout point," Washta said.

Then they heard squeals.

All three rushed in the direction of the noise, walking quite a distance, passing several trees.

"Are we still climbing?" Michelle asked. "It feels like we are."

The squealing was getting louder, and they heard a lot of rustling noise.

Then they saw it.

"Oh, look at that!" Michelle said. "The mink is fighting a muskrat. Are they really fighting, or are they just playing?"

"They are fighting," Washta said. "But I know the mink is the strongest."

"It's sad to see animals fight," Michelle said. "Even an ugly rat."

"Is there something going on over there?" David asked, pointing to a dark puff of smoke floating in the air above the hill not too far in the distance.

Both Michelle and Washta looked up at the sky.

"Only one puff so far," David said.

"That's how we communicate," Washta said, focused on the sky. "One puff means to pay attention, something is going on."

"No, there is another puff," Michelle said.

"This means everything is OK," Washta said. "I am wondering why the Oglala tribe is sending these signals."

"Should we be concerned?" David asked.

"I don't think so," Washta said. "Someone is probably just saying hi."

"But wait! There is a third puff," Michelle said.

"Well, that means something is going on," Washta said, looking a little preoccupied.

"Are we going to be attacked?" Michelle asked in a scared, halting voice.

"Nothing is coming from our side," Washta said. "So I think we will be OK. I'll keep my eyes on the sky. If there are more signals, we will head back to the village."

Taka was still not around.

"Taka! Taka!" Washta called out. "Unusual for him, but he will be back soon, I am sure."

The wolf was nowhere in sight.

11

The Gigantic Spider Web

All of a sudden, the sky became dark with menacing clouds.

"Rain is coming," Washta said. "I'd like Taka to be right by my side. There are so many predators around."

"There's Taka!" David said, pointing to the red wolf standing by a cave.

All three rushed toward Taka but were stopped by a huge spider web spread from one tree to another, spanning forty feet wide, blocking their way.

Washta immediately stopped running. He put his hands out, barring Michelle and David from moving forward.

"I have never seen such a big spider web," Washta said. "We cannot walk through this. There is a reason the web is in our way."

"Neither have we," David said.

"Wow!" Michelle exclaimed. "Is this really a spider web?"

"Look at the spider in the middle of this huge web," David said in awe.

"Wow!" Michelle exclaimed. This huge spider web was wider than her bedroom at home. "Is this really a spider web?"

"Yes," Washta answered.

"Don't you see the spider in the middle?" David said, pointing it out.

"I think Iktomi, the spider spirit, is telling us something," Washta said. "It is telling us to stay away from something. It is protecting us."

"Protecting us from what?" Michelle asked, looking nervously around.

"I don't know," Washta said. "Let's keep our eyes open."

"Shall we walk right through the web?" David asked.

"No, there is a reason the web is there," Washta repeated. "That would be to destroy something Mother Earth is giving us."

"Then what do you suggest we do?" David asked.

Washta didn't have to reply because at that moment, an antelope, pursued by a mountain lion, came running through the web, leaving a big opening and destroying part of the web.

The antelope was scared of the big, ferocious, hungry mountain lion, who only had eyes for its prey. Both were totally oblivious to the kids. One wanted to eat, and the other one didn't want to get eaten.

"OK," Washta said once the mountain lion and the antelope had disappeared. "Now we can go through the opening of the web. Let's go."

12

The Popcorn Cave

They went through the large web opening and continued on their way to the cave ahead of them, walking very carefully.

"Washta, look on the branch! I see a little black bear sleeping," David muttered very low so as not to wake the bear.

"It's beautiful," Michelle said. "It looks like a giant teddy bear stretched out on a branch."

"Let's quietly get away from here," Washta said in a very low voice. "We don't want to have a bear come after us."

All three ran as quietly and as fast as they could away from the bear.

"Where are we going?" Michelle asked, keeping her eyes on the bear, who wasn't moving.

"Just follow me," Washta answered. "I know this area inside and out. I come here often."

"So, you have seen bears here before?" Michelle asked.

"To tell you the truth, I haven't seen many," Washta said. "They usually stay away from here, but once in a while, I see one." Washta was not telling the whole truth. His father had told him that bears did like to hibernate in the caves and to be careful when coming this way.

"It's raining," Michelle said, feeling a few drops falling on her face and looking at her precious red shoes. "We are going to get all wet."

"Let's go back to the village," David said.

"Too late. The rain won't last long," Washta said. "But let's take shelter in the cave straight ahead before it pours."

The rain started coming down pretty hard when they entered the small cave.

"Wow!" David said, looking up at the ceiling. "Are there lots of caves with ceilings like this?"

"I think so," Washta said, looking around the inside of the cave to see if it was safe, indifferent to the popcorn formation. "I have only seen this one, but I have heard people talk about other caves with those kinds of ceilings."

"There is a lot of grass here, as if something has been sitting or sleeping here," David said, pointing at the grass on the ground.

"Hmmm," Washta said. He spit into his hands and then rubbed them on the grass.

"What are you doing?" Michelle asked, disgusted.

"I want to see if a bear has been here," Washta said, looking at his hands. "Yep, a bear has been here. Look at the dark hairs sticking to my hand."

"Amazing," David said, looking at the dark hair on Washta's hand. "That's a very good way to find out."

"A bear!" Michelle said.

"Bears," David said with his eyes wide open.

"Now, what do we do if one surprises us in here?" Michelle asked.

"Bears explore many areas before deciding where to spend the winter," Washta said. "This cave has always been a good place for bears or bobcats or foxes."

"That doesn't sound safe to me," Michelle said.

"Don't worry, Michelle," David said. "I have a way to get out of here if we are in danger."

"I hope you know what you are doing," Michelle said.

Washta looked outside and saw the rain had already stopped. He turned around to see David touch the boxwork made of thin blades of calcite forming a honeycomb pattern on the cave's wall.

"The rain stopped," Washta said. "The clouds are gone. We can get going. We will be OK for a while. David, what are you looking at?"

"I have been in caves with stalagmites before, but this is the first time I've seen these honeycomb boxes," he replied, intrigued by the thin blades forming boxes like the cardboard formation inside boxes that securely hold bottles in place. "These are cool," he added.

"They look like cardboard box dividers in boxes," Michelle said. "It's very interesting to look at."

"Yes, they are," Washta said in a detached voice. "There is a most unique sacred wind cave a few days' walk from here. Those boxwood and frostwork formations are all over that cave. This is nothing compared to what's in that cave."

"Why is it called a wind cave?" Michelle asked.

"Very simple," Washta said. "When someone walks by the entrance, there is strong wind blowing out of it. It can blow you off the ground."

"Wow! I'd like to see that," David said. "I wish we could go to that mysterious whistling cave," he added, very intrigued.

"Me too," Michelle said.

13

The Badger and the Bobcat Tug-of-War

"Let's get to the lookout point before it rains again," Washta said, pointing to a narrow serpentine trail in the distance.

As they were stepping out of the cave, an unexpected event was taking place.

Right in front of them, the small black bear was climbing down the tree, disturbed by all the raucous sounds close by.

"Itko!" screamed Washta, recognizing his pet. "Come over here!"

"What's going on?" David asked, coming out of the cave with Michelle in tow.

"Oh, my God!" Michelle uttered, looking at the animals in front of her.

"The bobcat wants the rabbit, and the badger won't let him have it," Washta said.

"Did you know that the hairs on a bobcat's ears act as an antenna and warn him when there is an enemy close by?" David said.

"He is also very territorial," Washta added.

"Now there is a bear with a bird in its mouth getting close to the bobcat," Michelle said, backing away from the scene.

"The bear dropped his bird and wants in on the action," David said as the bear nonchalantly approached the determined badger, who was pulling the rabbit, and the jumpy bobcat, who didn't want to let it go. The small badger was tugging and tugging at the rabbit, and no matter how hard the easygoing but nervous bobcat tried to get the rabbit all for itself, it just didn't have the strength, nor did it want to get into a fight with the growling badger.

The bear at the scene spooked the jumpy bobcat.

"The bear is making the bobcat nervous," Washta said.

"Poor bobcat," Michelle said.

"The badger's angry growls are also scaring the bobcat," David said as the bobcat gave up on the rabbit. It had had enough and left the badger and the bear to themselves.

The bear went to the badger, who growled at it.

"Is the bear going to be intimidated by the badger too?" Michelle asked.

"It looks like he doesn't like the growling badger either," Washta said. "He's got a bird anyways that he can go back to."

The bear had dropped the bird to examine the bobcat and the badger and now had nothing. The bear looked around for more exciting things to do. When he saw the kids, he walked toward them.

"The bear is coming at us!" Michelle cried. "What do we do?"

"Let's stand still for a minute," Washta said, stopping right then. "Don't worry; it will go away." Pointing to the sky, he added, "Look what's coming."

A golden eagle with a fish in its mouth came flying down. It dropped the fish at the bear's feet and nipped the bear's shoulder on its way down. It flew up a little and dived down, nipping the bear's shoulder again and again.

"The bear has got a fish to play with," David said, laughing.

"Is the eagle trying to distract the bear?" Michelle asked.

"Yeah. Let's go," Washta ordered, walking quickly away from the small bear, who, for the time being, was distracted. "This is a hint. We need to get away from here as fast as we can."

"Are we going back to the village?" Michelle asked.

"Not yet," Washta answered. "I need to go to the lookout point for a few minutes and check if there is any activity down below in the valley."

"Why?" David asked.

"I need to see if there are any buffalo," Washta said. "It's my chore. I do this every day."

They walked away as fast as they could, leaving the eagle to keep an eye on the bear with the fish and the badger with the rabbit.

14

The Lookout Point

They walked silently on a trail cut through groves of trees, sometimes even walking very close to the edge of a cliff. The drop was hundreds of feet down. They carefully looked all around to make sure there would be no more animal surprises. Then, after they had passed a series of petrified stumps and short bushes, the trail ended. They were on top of a small hill overlooking a majestic green valley with a stream running through and animals grazing everywhere.

"This is the lookout point," Washta said.

"This view is incredible," Michelle said, sitting down to look at all the activity going on below them.

"Michelle, did you see the wild horses?" David asked, knowing she loved horses.

"Of course," Michelle said. "They are just as beautiful as the horses I have at home. These are mustangs, you know."

There were a lot of animals she didn't know the name of, so she was proud to be able to identify the mustangs.

"Isn't it incredible how many wild horses there are?" David said. "Look at the pronghorn antelope grazing along with them while others are running and trying to compete with the horses."

"What do you think happened to the millions of wild horses?" Michelle asked. "There are only a few thousand left now."

"Didn't Mrs. Savant say a million horses were assigned to combat during the Civil War," David said. "The ranchers also killed a lot of wild horses for meat or sport. I don't think they thought much of them."

"How sad! There are certainly a lot down there," Michelle replied. "Washta, what are you doing now?"

"My job is to come up here not only to watch for buffalo but to check to see if everything is quiet down there and not threatening our village," Washta said. "I thought you might enjoy the walk here."

"That was exciting," Michelle said. "I loved it."

"From here, have you seen enemies come close, wanting to do battle with your village?" David asked.

"Not very often, if not for the Chippewa," Washta answered. "The Chippewa are very greedy and want all the land you see for themselves. So they fight with us to force us to evacuate the land."

"When is the last time they were here?" David asked.

"A few moons ago," Washta answered. "It has been quiet for a while."

"Have you ever seen buffalo?" Michelle asked.

"Oh! Yes, a while back!" Washta answered. "They are fun to watch. Buffalo wander around here because there is a lot of grass to graze on and because there is water close by. I have seen two hundred buffalo follow a leader to the water stream. And once they drink, they rest before they leave, wandering and moving to look for other fresh fields to graze on. It's quite a sight."

"What do you do once you spot a herd?" David asked.

"I immediately go alert the camp," Washta said. "We always need fresh buffalo meat. Our survival depends on the gentle buffalo, but they are becoming rarer. There used to be buffalo coming this way almost daily. The whole plain would be black with buffalo. It has been three weeks since I have seen any buffalo."

"Maybe we will be lucky and see some today," Michelle said.

"I have a feeling we will," Washta said. "They are due to show up. They haven't been around for a long time. The grass is high and fresh. And that's what they are looking for."

"How about the herds of antelope and elk?" David asked. "Are they as important as the buffalo?"

"They are important too, but we depend on the buffalo more," Washta said. "We can't do as much with the elk and the antelope. We use every part of the buffalo, and we can't do that with the elk or the antelope."

"Look how fast the antelope are running," Michelle said, pointing at the speeding antelope.

"Only the cheetah runs faster than the antelope," David said. "They love to race and outdo other animals."

"What's a cheetah?" Washta asked.

"It's a very big cat with black spots on gold fur," David answered.

"I have never seen them," Washta said. "Where did you see them?"

"I have never seen one," David said. "I only heard about them."

"Look at what the antelope are doing," Michelle said. "They are forming an oval formation just like that flock of birds flying above us."

David and Washta looked at the gray sky, and not only did they see birds forming a V formation but a golden eagle flying across the river.

"What a beautiful eagle!" David said. "Is that the same eagle we saw earlier?"

"Could be," Washta said.

"Before I came here, I had only seen them in zoos," Michelle said. "They are so beautiful flying."

"The eagle is sending us another message," Washta said.

"Is that good or bad?" Michelle asked.

"It's a good sign," Washta said. "We will see buffalo; I am sure."

All three looked in the direction of the eagle smoothly gliding through the air. It persisted in flying around and around as if it was calculating its descent, preparing for a move, having seen something it was ready to get.

"What do you think the eagle is looking for?" David asked.

"Let's go find out," Washta said.

"Look! I see something moving in the trees across the river," Michelle said excitedly. "It's a buffalo."

"No, you didn't," David said, looking across the river. "I don't see anything."

"I am telling you I saw a buffalo," Michelle said.

"Maybe you did," Washta said, now running down the hill toward the river. "Let's go check it out."

"I still don't see any buffalo," David said, running after Washta.

"I am sure I saw a buffalo," Michelle reasserted, following David.

"It can't be a buffalo because they move in groups," David said.

"They do move in groups unless they are old and can't keep up," Washta said. "Actually the young bull likes to do his own thing too, and he often strays from the group. If you saw a buffalo, it could be a bull."

"I see it again," Michelle said, running too.

But David and Washta didn't see it.

"There is definitely something going on across the river," Washta said, rushing downhill. "Even though I can't see what it is."

15

The Special Yipping Show

"Guess who's back?" David yelled. "Washta, look!"

Washta stopped, turned around, and saw Taka running toward him. He waited for him.

"Taka, there you are," Washta said, ruffling the wolf's fur. "Did you find your little brother?"

The wolf just wagged his tail.

"You're just in time," Washta said, looking at Taka. "We're going on a little scouting mission. Let's get going."

Washta resumed his run. Michelle's question didn't stop him.

"David, did you hear that loud sound?" she asked, pulling David's sleeve to stop him. "It sounded like a cry."

"I heard lots of sounds," David said.

"Won't you stop for a minute and listen?" Michelle said.

"Come on, Michelle," David said. "I don't want to stop. Let go of my sleeve."

"Here, I hear yips, growls, barks, and chirps," Michelle said, releasing David's sleeve, bumping into him, and tripping him by accident. "I am not imagining...Something is chirping and wheezing. Listen..."

They both fell on the ground to the quizzical looks of hundreds of black-tailed prairie dogs, chirping louder and standing by holes in the ground.

"Wow!" Michelle uttered in delight. "I have never seen those before. Funny-looking squirrels. Oh! Look! They are standing up and kissing each other."

"Those are not squirrels," David said, laughing.

"What are you two doing flat on your stomachs?" Washta shouted, turning around one more time but continuing on his descent. "Oh! I see. You are looking at prairie dogs. They are funny to look at, aren't they?"

"Prairie dogs!" Michelle exclaimed.

"Yep and they are not kissing each other," David said. "They are greeting each other by touching noses. They are very social animals, and if you are quiet, you will hear an all-clear call and see a funny thing happen."

Everyone was quiet, even Taka, who ran calmly by Washta.

The silence lasted a few minutes. Even the prairie dogs stood at attention. Then a prairie dog yipped and jumped.

"The *yip* told the prairie dogs that they are safe," David whispered. "Watch what they do."

All of a sudden, a big, loud party erupted. All the prairie dogs were yipping and jumping.

Michelle started clapping and laughing, and so did David.

"Quite a show!" Michelle exclaimed, getting up.

"Washta is way ahead of us," David said. "Let's go catch up with him."

The minute David and Michelle started moving, the prairie dogs hurried away into their burrows.

"The show is over," Michelle said.

They both ran down to join Washta, who was now standing by some men who were making canoes.

16

Michelle Gets Hurt

Michelle and David ran to Washta, all excited to see canoes.

"It would be so much fun to ride in a canoe," Michelle told David. "I have never been in a canoe. Wouldn't you like to ride in one?"

"That would be fun," David agreed.

They were fascinated by the canoes. David spotted a man way up a tree with an adze.

"What's he doing up a tree?" David asked, pointing to the Lakota man in the tree.

"He is slicing bark off the trunk to make a *kenu*," Washta said.

"A *kenu*?" Michelle asked.

"A *canoe*," David translated, elongating the word.

The man came down and with the help of another picked up the bark, rolled it up, and carried it close to the sandy river's edge. There they unrolled the bark and poured hot water on it.

"Why are they pouring hot water on the bark?" David asked Washta.

"The water softens the bark and makes it easier to work with it," Washta said.

"What are they doing?" David asked, watching the men split pieces of wood into long, thin strips.

"They are making strips that are going to be used for lining the inside of the canoe," Washta answered as the men laid the strips of wood on the bark. "The strips of wood protect the bark as the canoe is being built."

Then one of them got two more long, fat pieces of wood and tied them together at both ends with raw bone threads.

"Washta, do you know how to build a canoe?" David asked.

"I am learning," Washta answered.

"Look at what they're doing now," Michelle said.

They were spreading apart the two long pieces of wood, placing a cross piece in the middle between the two long pieces, and tying each side.

"They are making the frame," Washta said. "See...They fitted two more cross pieces and put them into place closer to each end."

"It does look like the perimeter of a canoe," Michelle said, proud of her use of the word *perimeter*.

The men next laid the frame on the bark and put heavy stones in the center of the bark.

"The stones keep the frame in place," Washta explained.

"What are they going to do next?" David asked as he watched the men walk to the end of the canoe frame now on top of the bark.

"They're going shape the canoe. First, they're going to fold the ends up and then hold them with a vise," Washta said.

"Interesting," David said, fascinated at seeing the canoe take shape.

"Now that both ends are up," Washta said. "They're going to do the side. But right now, the bark is too stiff to handle. They need to prepare the side and make it flexible before lifting it."

"I know how they're going to do that," Michelle said. "They're going to pour hot water on the bark all the way around."

"Exactly! And the water will keep the bark from splitting," Washta said as a man continuously poured hot water on the bark. "Next, they will lift the bark with a stick."

Michelle and David watched as the men carefully lifted the bark up on the frame at the front and at the back of the canoe in the making.

"Super cool!" David exclaimed.

They walked to the end of the frame, folded the ends up, lifted up the bark, and held it in place with a vise. They then again poured hot water on the bark all along the frame, lifting it slightly with a stick.

"Now, the bark needs to stay up," Washta said as the men pushed sticks into the ground all around the canoe. "They put sticks all along the frame. That keeps the side up."

They were done anchoring sticks all along the frame between the ends.

"Almost done," Washta said.

"It doesn't look done to me," Michelle said, examining the gap between the ends. "Some bark is missing."

"Give it time," Washta said, as they watched the men pick up some more bark and bring it back to the canoe.

"I'd love to help build a canoe," David said. "Do the men need help?"

"Hmm," Washta answered, not sure the men would welcome their help. "The bark is light even though wet. Yeah, let's go give them a hand. I think that's OK."

"I see," Michelle said, watching the men add bark to complete one side of the canoe.

All three walked to the canoe. Washta said something to the men, who nodded. Washta then instructed David and Michelle to help the men hold the bark as they gently laid it on the opposite side.

All three helped the men hold the bark and carefully set it down. The men pushed the sticks close the side of the canoe.

"We're done," Washta said, looking at Michelle and David.

"That was fun," David said, backing away from the canoe.

Both men smiled at them and went back to working on other canoes. Now it was the women's turn to work on the canoe.

"Look! There's your mom," Michelle said, waving at Washta's mom, who was approaching the canoe with other women.

The smiling women were holding thin ropes.

"What are the women going to do with the ropes?" Michelle asked.

"The most tedious task," Washta said. "Now they sew all the seams together with the sinews—or ropes, as you call them."

"Do they use a needle?" Michelle asked.

"A needle?" Washta said in surprise. "They use a buffalo bone."

"It looks like a big needle to me," Michelle stated.

"They need a big buffalo awl or strong needle to thread those cords through the sturdy bark," David commented.

"There are buffalo sinews," Washta said. "But not all cords are buffalo sinews."

"The sinews look like very thick threads or cords to us," Michelle said.

"Threads? I don't know what you mean by *threads*," Washta said. "There are also spruce roots that the men pulled from the ground. After that, they carefully split the roots and soaked them in water to make them soft while other cords come from the buffalo."

"Look at the women," Michelle told David. "They're punching holes in the seams."

"Yes," Washta said. "They go from the front to the back of the canoe, punching holes and pushing the spruce thread through with a pointed bone."

"Incredible those bone awls!" Michelle said. "The holes have to be big for the women to push the ropes through."

"How about the spruce threads," David said. "How would you even think of spruce producing threads!"

"I would never have thought of a tree producing threads," Michelle said. "Actually heavy ropes."

"It must take forever for the women to punch holes all the way around," David said.

"It does take time," Washta acknowledged. "But a group of women can do it fast."

"And pushing the thread through the bark must be even harder," Michelle said.

"It's not easy," Washta admitted. "They have done this for years."

"Why is that man bending a piece of wood?" David asked as he was watching a man bend a piece of wood a little.

"He's making the front of the canoe," Washta said.

"But how does the wood stay curved?" Michelle asked.

"A man wraps the wood with bark strings and attaches it to the front of the frame of the kenu and another one at the back of the frame," Washta said. "After they finish wrapping it, they'll trim the bark to make it efficient."

"Why is the man cutting more bark at the front?" Michelle asked. "I thought he was done."

"A little adjustment to make the canoe split the water quietly, easily, and quickly," Washta answered.

"It looks so easy to make a canoe," David observed as the canoe was taking shape.

"As long as you know what you're doing," Washta said. "The canoe needs to be well built because it has to hold up to twelve people without sinking."

"Isn't the water going to leak in through the holes that the women punched?" Michelle asked.

"No," Washta answered. "The women will seal each hole with spruce gum and tallow."

"Clever," David answered. "Using the gooey stuff that comes out of a spruce tree wound."

"Really clever," Michelle repeated. "Using the sap from the tree. When we get home, we should try using the sap to plug holes in a bottle to see if it works or leaks."

"Good idea, Michelle," David said.

They both watched the women plug the holes.

"Do you think it really makes the canoe waterproof?" Michelle asked, unconvinced.

"I'm sure it does," David answered. "Indians have been doing this forever."

Washta went to his mom and asked her about the smoke signals he had seen earlier.

After a few seconds of reflection, Michelle blurted out, "Can we go on a canoe ride?"

"That would be fun," David said. "How about fishing from a canoe?"

"No, really! You want to go fishing?" Michelle asked. "On a canoe?"

"Sure. Why not?" David asked.

"Come on, David," Michelle retorted. "This boat isn't stable enough for anyone to stand and throw a line from it. Plus I don't feel like fishing."

"The canoe is well-balanced. You just need to be calm and stay centered in your seat so the canoe doesn't tip," David suggested.

"Well," Michelle said. "There you go. How can you stay in your seat motionless if you fish?"

"Oh, I can," David said.

"I'm surprised you would want to fish," Michelle said, crossing her arms. "You never can stay still. How about we go fishing some other time? I'd love to go canoeing without doing anything else."

~

Washta had not had time to put his two cents in. He was watching Taka. Taka had run to the edge of the river and disappeared.

Washta walked to the edge of the river, looking for him.

"Taka! Taka, where are you going?" Washta said, looking all over for Taka.

David and Michelle went to find Washta.

"Where did Taka go?" David asked. "Did he go across the river?"

"I don't think so," Washta said, trying to get a glimpse of where Taka might be hiding. "He must be chasing something in a bush close by."

Then they heard loud growling and howling across the river. Taka reappeared from behind some bushes and came running back toward Washta.

"There he is!" David shouted.

Taka, even though a wolf, was a scaredy-cat. He was always jittery at the sound of loud barking or howling. After a few seconds, he went back and forth between Washta and the shore, as if he wanted to say something.

"It's OK, Taka," Washta said, trying to reassure Taka. "It sounds like it's one of your cousins howling."

"What's going on?" David asked, excited at this new turn of events.

"Taka is nervous," Washta answered. "He heard grunting, snorting, and growling. That spooked him. I have a feeling Michelle was right. There are buffalo close by. And I heard a wolf howling. Could be Itko."

"I told you at the lookout point I saw a buffalo," Michelle said. "We forgot all about it when we saw the canoes."

"Does Taka think that Itko is howling to warn of danger?" David asked.

"Yes," Washta replied. "But that wouldn't spook Taka."

"Ouch!" Michelle screamed in pain. "I stepped on a bone awl. I was too busy looking across the river and I wasn't looking where I was going." She removed the little bone awl from her red shoe.

"How did this happen?" David asked in surprise. "Why did you wear your fancy shoes? You should have been wearing boots or gym shoes."

"I am wearing my Mary Jane slippers," Michelle said. "They are very thin. Had I known we would be coming here, I would have worn my boots." Michelle was annoyed at putting a hole in her beautiful shoe.

"Let's go closer to the edge of the river and take a look," Washta said. "We'll put water on your serious wound." He was amused.

The group, including Taka, left the women working on the canoe and walked a few feet to the edge of the river where some canoes were gently rocking.

Michelle went to one and hanging on to its side took her shoes off. She looked at her foot and said, "It is just a little puncture. I'll live." She then climbed into the canoe and sat carefully in it, letting her legs hang out in the water.

"The water's not bad," Michelle said, gently dancing her legs in and out of the water.

"Michelle, how am I going to look at your foot?" David asked. "You're too far from me. I'm not getting wet."

"You don't have to," Michelle replied. "I'm fine."

Washta, however, wanted to take a look. He walked into the shallow water to where Michelle was.

"I want to see," Washta said with concern. "Show me your foot."

Michelle straightened her foot, pulling it out of the water. Washta looked at it carefully and threw more water on it.

"It's nothing," Washta said confidently. "Just a little poke."

"Thank you," Michelle said. "But that's exactly what I said. I nevertheless appreciate your concern."

17

A Man Chases a Buffalo Chasing Itko Chasing a Mole

All of a sudden, they heard a plop. Taka was in the river, swimming across the narrow strip of water.

"Look at Taka swimming across the river!" Michelle said excitedly.

Washta turned. "Taka, what's up?" he asked surprised by Taka's sudden move. "Where are you going?"

Taka didn't listen.

"What did he see?" Michelle asked, putting her legs in the canoe and slipping her shoes back on. She slowly and carefully stood up and looked in Taka's direction.

Washta came to stand by David. All three were scrutinizing the river when something caught their attention.

On the opposite side of the river, there was a lot of noise and branches were moving.

"Look! There's the buffalo!" Michelle shouted, almost losing her balance and making the canoe rock violently and frenetically.

Washta quickly returned to the canoe, got in the water, and steadied it.

"Go ahead, Michelle. Jump out," Washta said. "I'm holding the canoe. You'll be fine."

David went to the front of the shaky canoe and helped Michelle get out without falling.

"Why did you go in the canoe in the first place?" David asked Michelle, annoyed.

"Why not?" Michelle replied. "So you know, I didn't want to sit on the ground and get my foot dirty. Everything worked out OK, didn't it?"

"Itko, what are you doing over there?" Washta asked.

"It's so funny watching Itko," Michelle said. "He's hopping like a rabbit, trying to get something."

"What's he chasing?" David asked.

"Itko, come on, boy! Come back here!" Washta yelled, hoping Itko would heed his call, but the little wolf was too busy chasing a mole.

"He got a mole," David observed. "But look what's chasing him."

Everyone stopped and ran to the bank of the river to watch the scene being played out across the river.

Some were laughing, some were not, but all were applauding Itko's prowess.

"Itko, watch out!" Washta was not amused and yelled as the buffalo came charging at him. But

Itko, busy with the little mole, ignored Washta's warning and kept digging.

The others watched Taka, who was already in the middle of the river, wondering what he was up to.

"Will Taka be able to make it to the other side?" Michelle asked.

"Wolves are good swimmers," David said. "He'll make it."

"Buffalo! Buffalo!" yelled the now excited small crowd that had gathered.

"Why don't you go check it out?" Washta's mom told him.

One of the Indians working on a canoe heard Wise Owl's plea to Washta. He came to Washta and pointing to his beautiful canoe resting in the water ready to go, said, "Listen to Wise Owl. Take my canoe. Go check for buffalo and get Itko."

"Thank you, Light Foot," Washta said. "I will."

Washta waved at David and Michelle to join him.

"Be careful," Wise Owl said. "You know how canoes can sometimes be treacherous."

All three got into the handsome canoe and were quickly on their way. The slick canoe cut through the water fast.

"Wow, I didn't realize how quick a canoe is!" Michelle exclaimed.

In no time, they were by Taka's side. But Washta didn't stop.

"You're almost there, Taka," Washta said, paddling fast while encouraging the little wolf along. "Let's go get Itko."

Washta continued to shore. David and Michelle sat very quietly even though a rugged-looking man with a ponytail had suddenly appeared. He was chasing after the buffalo, trying to get ahold of a saddle that was hanging on its side.

David couldn't stay still or hold his tongue any longer and asked, "Why is there a saddle on the buffalo? People can't ride a buffalo, can they?"

"Nobody I know has ever tried to," Washta answered.

The canoe started to sway side to side.

"Stop moving!" Michelle said, hanging on tightly to the side of the canoe. "You're going to make us tip over!"

"It's the first time I've seen a saddle on a buffalo," Washta said, perplexed. "I am not sure why there is a saddle on this buffalo. Buffalo are dangerous and can kill you."

They landed safely on the shore.

Washta and David were so impatient to get out that they forgot how easily the canoe could overturn.

Washta was the first to get out of the canoe.

The man stopped the buffalo by grabbing the buffalo's leash.

"Why bother with this wolf?" the buffalo man asked the buffalo. "It didn't care about you. All it wanted was the mole."

As if the buffalo understood, it stood there quietly, watching Itko eat the mole.

18

Theodore Roosevelt to the Rescue

As David was getting off, the canoe started slipping back into the water. It swayed back and forth, freaking Michelle out.

Michelle screamed, "David, help!"

Even though the slim canoe was partly on dry land, she was afraid of moving because the shaky canoe might tip and she would fall into the water. The last thing she wanted was to ruin her special red shoes.

David had jumped out quickly and run toward Washta just as a thin young man wearing a fur hat with a long tail hanging from the back, having heard the desperate scream, rushed toward the runaway and unstable canoe.

David didn't want to miss the opportunity to see this subdued buffalo held on a leash, just like one would hold a dog.

"Look at this huge, complacent buffalo!" David shouted, not turning to see Michelle's situation. "I can't miss getting close to it."

Michelle watched helplessly as David nonchalantly bent down, picked up something from the ground, and resumed his furious dash toward the buffalo. She yelled, "David, why did you jump without warning me? You could have warned me!"

Nervously hanging on tightly to the side of the canoe, she continued, "Look at the canoe slipping. I could fall in the water, or worse, I could drift away. Don't you care?"

"Let me help you get out," the serious-looking man said. He had a moustache and was wearing glasses. He grabbed hold of the unsteady canoe.

David had impulsively vaulted out of the canoe. In his hurry to get a look at the buffalo, he had forgotten all about Michelle and the canoe. *Well*, he thought, *Michelle can handle the canoe.*

"There. Problem solved," said the man, who was dressed in buckskin pants and a fancy cowboy shirt with a handkerchief around his neck. "Everything is good. The canoe won't drift. You won't fall. The canoe has stopped shaking and is back firmly on the ground. You can safely get out. I'll hold on to the canoe."

David forgot his desire to see the buffalo and came back to rescue his friend, but the man with the glasses had already saved the day.

"I'm sorry, Michelle," David said. "I didn't think. I thought you would be right behind me and would be able to jump like I did."

"I would have been able to," Michelle replied, "if the canoe had not been shaken when you leaped off so fast."

"It's OK. I'm here now," David said as he helped Michelle get off the canoe. "No harm done, no need to be upset." He had been too busy reassuring Michelle to pay attention to the man who was keeping the canoe in balance.

Michelle, ignoring David, looked at the unusual man and said, "Thank you, sir, for rescuing me."

David was about to say to Michelle, "How about thanking *me* for helping?" but stopped short as he recognized the man with the fancy cowboy clothes. "You are...You are..." David stuttered. He just couldn't get ahold of himself. He was in awe and stood there with his mouth wide open, unable to say anything.

"Theodore Roosevelt," the young man with the cowboy clothes said, laughing. "Nice to meet you both."

"Theodore Roosevelt! No, it can't be..." Michelle wasn't shy and shouted out excitedly, recognizing the dynamic man who had been the twenty-sixth president of the United States. "Wow! I can't believe it! You were...You are the..." Michelle stopped because she felt a kick in a leg. She yelled, "Ouch!"

David quickly shot Michelle a look, telling her to shut up and not reveal something that had not happened yet and would be hard to explain.

"Are you OK, little girl?" Teddy Roosevelt asked Michelle, who had just let out a scream of pain.

"Yes," Michelle said, rubbing her leg. "And my name is Michelle by the way." Michelle didn't like being called "little girl." "And this is David."

"Honor to meet you both." Theodore Roosevelt chuckled.

"It is an honor for us, sir," David said and smiled widely while frantically searching in his pocket for a treasure to share with Roosevelt. "What a treat to meet you in person!"

After rifling through his pocket furiously, David felt a giant water bug. He proudly took the four-inch insect out of his pocket and presented it to Roosevelt.

"Have you ever seen such a big bug?" David asked. "I just found it a few minutes ago on my way to see the buffalo. I would love for you to have it."

Roosevelt took the dead water bug, examined it, and said, "Beautiful specimen. I used to collect all kinds of insects and animals and still do when I have time."

"I know we heard you are a great collector," Michelle said. "David is too."

"You are, heh?" Roosevelt said, looking at the little blond kid who reminded him of himself. "Then why don't you keep it for your collection?"

David looked sad. Was Roosevelt rejecting his humble gift?

Roosevelt saw David's face and quickly said, "It's a pretty amazing-looking bug. I don't think I have one quite like this in my collection. So if you really want to part with it, I'll accept it and add it to my collection."

David's face lit up instantly.

"Now, tell me, what are you two young people doing in South Dakota Indian territory?" Roosevelt asked, gently wrapping the bug in his handkerchief before putting it in his pocket. "Your water bug will be part of my special collection."

"We are here learning all there is to know about Indians," David said.

"It's been incredible fun so far," Michelle said. "Do you know a lot about Indians?"

"Just like you, I am learning a lot too," Roosevelt said. "Look what's coming out of the water."

At that moment, Taka came out of the water and shook the water out of his fur. David abruptly left Michelle and Roosevelt and ran to Taka.

"Taka, you're such a good dog," David said, petting the wolf.

"Sorry, Mr. Roosevelt, you have to excuse David," Michelle said. "He is usually pretty polite, but he wants to make sure Taka is all right. You see, Taka is looking for his brother and crossed the river by himself hoping to find him."

"I see," Roosevelt said seriously. "I understand. I would do the same."

Both walked toward the very wet, barking puppy.

"Washta, look who just arrived! Washta! Washta! Taka is here," David shouted, looking for Washta, who had disappeared behind the tall grass. "He is sniffing the ground like crazy."

"He must be smelling Itko," Michelle said.

"Hold on to him!" Washta yelled from behind the trees. "I'll be right back. I'm looking to see if there are any buffalo roaming close by."

19

David Is Walking on Cloud Nine

"Who is Washta?" Roosevelt asked, trying his hardest to get a glimpse of Washta, who was somewhere past the tall grass, but it was too hard to see.

"Washta is our friend who lives across the river," David answered, pointing at the canoes and tepees across the river.

"His chore is to look for buffalo," Michelle added. "We came to help him."

"That's a very important job," Roosevelt said. "But he won't find any. I have been looking for buffalo for days."

"How could this be? We saw one just a few minutes ago," Michelle said, looking at the buffalo suddenly reappearing. But this time, a man was riding it.

"Let me correct that," Roosevelt said. "You're right. There is one buffalo around, but a man brought it here."

"Remember, Michelle, what our teacher said," David whispered. "Millions of buffalo were killed to force the Indians onto reservations. There aren't many buffalo left."

She nodded, confirming she had heard David, who had whispered in a voice barely audible so as not to attract the attention of Roosevelt. Roosevelt would want to know about their teacher, and David didn't want to get into it.

"Look!" she said, pointing to the huge brown-haired animal with horns. "There's the buffalo again."

"How does he do that?" David asked, dumbfounded. "Ride a buffalo, I mean. I thought buffalo were dangerous."

"I was thinking the same thing. How can anyone ride a buffalo?" Michelle concurred. "Aren't buffalo dangerous?"

"You're right. Buffalo are dangerous," Roosevelt said. "This buffalo is an exception though. Charlie 'Buffalo' Jones was able to tame one enough to ride it everywhere safely."

"I want to find out how he did it," David said. "Let's go see the man with the buffalo."

"Yes, let's do," Roosevelt said. "He is probably around the tent we set up."

"I don't see a tent," David said, looking around.

"Me neither," Michelle agreed.

"It's there. I got caught in the rain and got all muddy, so I decided to set up camp close by behind the trees over there," Roosevelt added, pointing to a group of trees. "Charlie Buffalo Jones had the same problem with the heavy rain. We met right on the spot where we set up the tents, and we both decided to wait out the rain."

"That's why you're covered with mud," Michelle said. "I was surprised to see you dirty. Every picture I saw of you showed you squeaky-clean."

"Really!" Roosevelt said, laughing. "A little dirt has never hurt anyone."

Taka couldn't be restrained any longer. He had heard Washta's voice and Itko's howl, which had spooked the buffalo in the first place and sent him on a gentle rampage, but Washta quickly brought Itko back under control. Taka, smelling Itko's scent, whimpered and left in the direction of the tents, not knowing of Roosevelt's comment.

"Why did Taka whimper and moan instead of howl?" Michelle asked.

Roosevelt was about to answer when David promptly interjected, "Wolves whimper when they feel insecure and need reassurance."

"I am impressed, young man," Roosevelt responded.

David was as happy as a lark. He had impressed the famous collector who, after all, had a natural history museum named after him.

Walking with his head up in the clouds, David stumbled on a branch covered with green bugs and fell face first into a pile of leaves, scaring the bugs in every direction.

"Look at you!" Michelle laughed as dozens of green treehoppers flew all around him, excited by the sudden arrival of this giant. Then an unexpected, beautiful giant black swallowtail, a cabbage white butterfly, and a candy-striped leafhopper emerged and joined the party.

"Wow!" Michelle said. "How did you do that?"

"What?" David asked.

"Have butterflies and the candy-striped leaf bugs appear," Michelle answered.

"Now, finally you know something about the animal world," David said.

"Surreal! And look at this green treehopper!" she exclaimed. "What an unusual insect it is! It looks like a green fish with legs," Michelle said.

"More like a tiny buffalo," said David, always the keen observer. He got up. "Don't you see the large head and the humpback? They are probably called buffalo hoppers."

"Kind of," said Michelle, not as sharp-eyed as David when it came to bugs.

"Those are called buffalo treehoppers," Roosevelt answered.

Again, David beamed.

"And look, David, you are covered with red twigs," Michelle said, trying to brush the twigs away.

David looked down and said impatiently, "Michelle, you have so much to learn. These are not twigs. They are walking sticks. Look! The things are walking."

"Wow!" Michelle said in awe. "The tiny twigs are moving."

"And there is a katydid too," Roosevelt added.

"It's incredible how colorful all these insects are," Michelle said.

"You want to see something else amazing?" Roosevelt said. "Follow me. They're right by the tents."

"What do you think he wants to show us?" Michelle whispered to David.

"I don't know," David whispered back. "But I'm sure it will be interesting."

"What do you think happened to Washta?" Michelle asked.

"He went looking for buffalo," David answered.

20

David's Snake Lands on Roosevelt

෴

David started walking, and all the critters deserted him, except one, which found its way into Michelle's hair.

David quickly grabbed the candy-striped leaf-hopper, accidentally pulling a few strands of Michelle's hair. She screamed again.

"What's wrong with you, David?" Michelle said, pouting, not knowing that David had pulled a bug out of her hair. "Now, you're pulling my hair?"

"Nothing is wrong," David said, showing her the remarkable red-and-light-blue bug. "This was in your hair."

"It's beautiful," Michelle said, all forgiven. She was amazed. "It looks like a candy cane. Is it still alive?"

"I'm not sure," David said. "I think I grabbed it too fast."

They both scrutinized the little hopper, but it wasn't moving.

"I'll put it in my new pouch," David said and carefully wrapped it before putting it in his bag. "I need to get more bugs from here," he added seriously.

"We're almost there," Roosevelt said, walking fast. He thought the children were keeping up with his pace as he pushed away the branches of many pine trees in his path.

He turned around and saw Michelle and David way behind. They were stooped over something, but he couldn't say what.

As he was going to speak, he saw Michelle give David a stick.

David took the stick, lowered it to the ground, and lifted it. Hanging on it was a wriggling black snake with three long yellow stripes.

"Mr. Roosevelt, look what David caught!" Michelle said excitedly. "It's as long as I am."

"It's quite a beaut," Roosevelt said, laughing. "What are you going to do with it?"

David and Michelle ran to Roosevelt to show him their prized possession.

Out of nowhere, Itko showed up and jumped on David, who, not expecting it, jerked up and let go of the stick. It went flying with the snake. And somehow, the yellow and black snake landed on Roosevelt's shoulder, to David's and Michelle's horror. Both stood there paralyzed, unable to say anything.

But Roosevelt was unperturbed. He loved snakes.

"That's one way to share," Roosevelt said, laughing.

Both Michelle and David relaxed. Roosevelt wasn't upset. They too started laughing.

"Do you think Itko is going to eat the snake?" Roosevelt asked, carefully removing the nervous snake from his shoulder and depositing it on the ground.

Itko was fascinated with the wriggling snake and wanted to play with it. He went up to it cautiously. The snake hissed, so he backed up to a safe distance. He approached the snake a few more times and then finally quickly got the snake's tail but released it. The snake quickly zigzagged away.

Itko followed it but soon lost interest and went to find Washta when he heard him laughing close by.

"Wolves don't eat snakes," Michelle said.

"You're almost right," David said. "As a rule, they don't, but on some occasions, they have been known to eat snakes."

"Right again, David," Roosevelt said.

Michelle was now starting to feel stupid and decided to show her knowledge the next time the opportunity presented itself. She knew a lot too. She just had not been able to show it. She had better grades than David in almost every subject except animal science. David was the best in school on that subject.

21

Roosevelt's Surprise

They followed Roosevelt to a small but bushy pine tree with branches extending to the ground. He moved some branches, and there, lying on a bed of pine needles, were some beautiful baby fawns.

"Amazing!" Michelle said, kneeling down to be closer the beautiful, motionless fawns, who were as small as kittens. "We saw bigger fawns earlier, but I couldn't touch them. This time, I'm going to."

David approached softly so as not to scare the fawns.

"The mom left them hidden here," Michelle said, petting the fawns gently. "She knew they would be safer without her. Her presence would attract predators. They blend well, and not moving keeps them from drawing attention."

"Very well said, Michelle," Roosevelt uttered. "You two are incredibly astute nature observers."

"Thank you," Michelle said, beaming.

The quiet moment didn't last long. There was movement by the tents.

"What's going on over there?" David asked, listening to noise coming from around and behind the tents.

"I hope the mom comes back," Michelle said, oblivious to the noise a few feet from her. "But she will be scared to come close if she sees Taka and Itko and the buffalo."

"And us," David added.

"Yes, she will return once we are all gone," Roosevelt said. "As a matter of fact, I was getting ready to leave here when I heard Michelle's desperate cry."

"Where are you going?" David asked inquisitively.

"Back to Chimney Butte," Roosevelt answered. "That's my ranch by the Little Missouri River."

"What do you do there?" Michelle asked.

"I just bought some cattle," Roosevelt answered. "Even though my ranch hands are in charge of the cattle, I like to take care of them too. I also have eight horses that need to be attended to."

"I love horses," Michelle said. "They are my favorite animals. They are so much fun to ride."

"I love them too," Roosevelt said. "You should come and visit. Even though there no children there, you might enjoy seeing all the animals on the ranch."

"We'd love to come," both said in unison.

"Do you hunt?" David asked, changing the subject. He had all kinds of animals except horses. He wasn't as fortunate as Michelle, who owned them, even though he felt lucky she let him ride with her sometimes.

"Yes, I came to hunt buffalo, but there aren't many left," Roosevelt answered. "So I hunt for antelope and deer. I love hunting."

"Why do you like hunting so much?" Michelle asked sadly. She didn't like seeing animals being killed.

"Hunting is a sport," Roosevelt said. "It brings one closer to nature. The qualities developed by the hunter are the qualities needed by the soldier. Soldiers keep a country safe. It builds strength of character, but that being said, I am against the senseless slaughter of animals. One time, I went on a hunt and didn't kill anything, so a guide tied a bear to a tree and told me to shoot it so I could say I had killed something, but I refused. I kill animals for food, but mostly for science, for the purpose of study."

"Interesting," Michelle said, unsure it made hunting right. "That story inspired a toymaker to call all the bears he made *teddy bears*."

Roosevelt didn't hear. "Yuck!" Roosevelt screamed. He had stepped in the horse's poop. He wasn't happy. "My boots stink," he said in disgust. He went to a branch lying on the ground and scraped as much as he could off. "That helped a little, but I still stink. I'll wash the rest off in a minute."

They left the little fawns and walked to the small campsite, which was right by the pine tree and the fawns. Roosevelt went to a basin of water and soaked the bottom of his boots in it as Michelle and David watched.

22

Meeting the Buffalo Man and His Buffalo

"Hey, what are you doing?" a man sitting on a buffalo asked, coming out of nowhere.

"I stepped in horse poop," Roosevelt answered. "I stink like crazy. Water should clean it up and get rid of the smell."

"Not good for those fancy boots of yours," the buffalo man said, laughing.

"Washta, what are you doing on the buffalo?" Michelle asked, shocked to see Washta sitting in front of Charlie Buffalo Jones and hanging on to the buffalo's hair.

"Just went for a ride," Washta said with a wide smile.

"That's where you went!" Michelle said. "We were wondering where you disappeared to."

"You are the buffalo man?" David said.

"Yep, I go by the name Buffalo Jones," the friendly buffalo man said. "Short for Charles Buffalo Jones."

"I have never heard of you," David said. "And yet, you must be the only man in the world who ever rode a buffalo—I mean, rides a buffalo."

"I reckon I am," Buffalo Jones replied.

"How does it feel riding a buffalo?" Michelle asked.

"Weird," Washta answered exuberantly. "Not as comfortable as sitting on a horse but still lots of fun."

"Aren't you afraid to fall off and be squished by its massive weight?" Michelle asked.

"No," Washta answered. "It never entered my mind."

"David, how heavy is a buffalo?" Michelle asked, anticipating David would know the answer. He knew answers to everything.

"Grown buffalo are about fifteen hundred pounds to two thousand pounds," David said.

"This one is about the weight of fifty-five coyotes," Washta said, petting the giant king of the plains.

"This buffalo seems different. He is so mellow," David said. "What made him that way? What's so special about this buffalo?"

"I raised this buffalo from the moment he was born," Buffalo Jones said. "And because of that, he doesn't know how to be an aggressive buffalo. But he does get spooked and will run away from whatever scares him, just like a doe gets scared of everything."

"How fast does he run?" Michelle asked.

"Almost as fast a horse," Buffalo Jones answered.

"Has your buffalo ever been angry?" David asked.

"Yes," Buffalo Jones answered. "When he feels threatened by another animal or if someone is shooting at him."

"Can you tell if he is getting angry?" Michelle asked.

"Yes, he will blat or bellow, and the hair on his back stands up," Buffalo Jones answered.

The buffalo man approached Roosevelt, David, and Michelle slowly.

Roosevelt petted the docile and loving bison.

David and Michelle watched, unsure if they should come any closer.

"This animal is a monumental beast," Michelle said. "He looks like a giant lion."

"The lion of the plains...I want to ride it," David said, excited. "It would be so much fun."

"Don't you dare go on that beast!" Michelle exclaimed. "Your mom wouldn't want you to."

"This bison is safe," David said. "Look! Washta rode it, and nothing happened."

"Don't go," Michelle said crossing her arms and pouting. "I don't want to be left alone."

"Come ride with me then," David said imperiously.

∽

Roosevelt was busy holding his horse, thinking, *Which will be spooked first? The bison or the horse?*

The imposing horse caught Michelle's attention. She approached Roosevelt.

"I love your horse," Michelle said. "It is beautiful. I love the carved saddle and the plaited bridle and the silver-inlaid bit. You must really care for your horse to give it such fancy apparel. What's his name?"

"Manitou," Roosevelt said.

"Great name," Washta said. "Manitou means great spirit."

"I am a very good rider," Michelle said, petting the horse. "Could I ride Manitou?"

"Maybe later," Roosevelt answered. "With a buffalo here, I'm not sure it would be a good idea. Let's see how Samson does around Manitou and all the noise."

"OK," Michelle said reluctantly. "But how about if I ride the horse in the plains away from Samson?"

"We'll see," Roosevelt answered.

Roosevelt talked to Manitou and hitched him to a tree close to the tent. The easygoing horse was very content grazing in the tall grass at his feet.

"Manitou looks so even-tempered," Michelle said, hoping to get a chance to ride the horse.

23

Roosevelt and the Buffalo

"Buffalo Jones, can we get a ride?" David asked, excited at the anticipation of riding a buffalo.

"Why couldn't you?" Michelle told David. "Washta got to ride it."

Michelle wanted to score a point for her best friend David, even though she wasn't sure riding a buffalo was a safe thing to do. She didn't want to stay by herself so she had no choice but to go along with David.

"Why not?" Buffalo Jones said, getting off the buffalo while holding the reins firmly. "But first, let's watch Roosevelt ride the buffalo. You will see how a newcomer can ride this buffalo without problems."

Roosevelt was caught off guard and looked at Buffalo Jones for a minute. He was dying to ride the buffalo. He had been so busy in the last few hours that the opportunity had not presented itself.

"Roosevelt, you haven't ridden the buffalo yet?" David asked, surprised.

"Not yet," Roosevelt said, happy to be asked to ride the buffalo and unafraid to do so. "OK," he said, not wanting to lose the opportunity. "Let's see what Samson and I can do together."

Roosevelt approached Samson and without difficulty, hopped on.

"He is all yours," Buffalo Jones said, giving him the reins.

Within seconds, Roosevelt was riding the buffalo like one would a thoroughbred, going fast and yelling, "Yip...yippee...whoopee...wee..."

He was having the time of his life, and so was the compliant buffalo, who didn't mind this impetuous, unrestrained, boisterous, crazy man on his back.

"It looks easy," David said. "I want to do this."

"You can't mean riding it by yourself," Michelle said.

"Of course," David replied, laughing.

Michelle and David were enjoying this incredible performance by the twenty-sixth president, who wasn't afraid of anything and behaved as if he could conquer everything.

"I don't remember Mrs. Savant ever saying Roosevelt rode a buffalo, do you?" Michelle asked David.

"I don't remember either," David answered. "Even though she is a teacher and she knows a lot, she can't know everything."

"Do you think he really did though?" Michelle asked.

"I'm sure he did," David said. "He wasn't afraid of anything, and he was always willing to learn. Didn't he say he would never have been president if it had not been for his experiences in North Dakota? So maybe he rode a buffalo and didn't brag about it."

"You're right," Michelle acknowledged. "He did love to challenge himself and didn't boast about his accomplishments. Maybe we don't know everything he did."

"He is my hero," David said. "I want to grow up to be just like him."

"But for now, let's just ride the buffalo like him," Michelle said, feeling a little less afraid to go on a buffalo ride.

"OK, with no fear," David said, looking into Michelle's eyes.

~

After a few more intense riding moments, a smiling, reinvigorated Roosevelt came back in one piece with Samson.

"I tired the buffalo," Roosevelt said, getting off the exhausted buffalo and giving the reins to Buffalo Jones. "He is going to be very mellow because I am sure he is exhausted. You'll be safe."

"Hey, Teddy, why don't you give me a hand," Buffalo Jones said, hopping on the buffalo. "The kids are dying to go for a ride. Unfortunately, Washta, there is not enough space for you."

Washta was sad not to go with his friends, but he understood it was too much for the buffalo to handle. He knew his friends would love riding it.

"OK," Roosevelt said hesitantly. "I know you raised the buffalo and the buffalo and I got along well, but he doesn't know the children. Is he going to be OK with them?"

"Sure, he will," Buffalo Jones said. "Otherwise, I wouldn't have suggested it. He was fine with Washta. The kids have to be super quiet and not show fear. Samson is as docile, gentle, and sweet as a puppy. They'll be safe."

"Can you be as quiet as possible?" Roosevelt asked the kids. "Mostly, don't panic if Samson starts misbehaving. Sometimes buffalo turn on a whim."

Michelle was trembling with fear again, but she nodded.

"Sure we will," David said. "We'll try not to panic if Samson acts up."

"OK then," Roosevelt said as he lifted both kids and sat them on the saddle in front of Buffalo Jones. Hang on tight to each other."

"I'll hang on tight to them," Buffalo Jones said.

"You are going to love it," Washta said. "It's so much fun. I'll keep Taka and Itko close by, away from Samson."

"This is not very comfortable," Michelle said, wriggling every which way as she tried to find just the right spot on the rugged saddle.

"Stop moving, Michelle," David said, sitting in front of Michelle. "We are only going for a short ride."

"We are not going for long," Buffalo Jones reiterated. "I'm sure you can put up with a little discomfort."

"I will be right here, should you need me," Roosevelt said, watching them go.

"Samson likes the open space," Buffalo Jones said. "Let's go in the prairie. Are we all ready?"

"Yes," the children said, all stoked but not really knowing what to expect.

24

Michelle and David Hanging On for Dear Life

They left in the direction opposite the river. For a while, the buffalo seemed content to go at a very slow pace.

"What do you think of the ride so far?" Buffalo Jones asked.

"Pretty swishy, like riding an elephant," Michelle said hesitantly. "Fun, but I prefer riding a horse."

"Not me. I love it just as much," David said. "We're never going to have the opportunity to ride a buffalo again, so let's make the most of it."

"And how do you do that?" Michelle asked sarcastically. "Make the most of it?"

David shrugged his shoulders.

"I admit horses are easier to ride," Buffalo Jones replied. "Well! Well! Look what we have coming!"

The wolves had decided to join the party and were quickly gaining on Samson.

"Itko, come back!" Washta yelled, running after the wild puppy. Sweet Taka followed close behind.

"Oh no!" Michelle exclaimed nervously. "All we need are wolves spooking the buffalo."

"Is Samson going to freak out?" David asked.

"He could get spooked a little," Buffalo Jones answered, holding the reins tighter. He wanted more control. "This is going to get exciting!" he exclaimed. "Hang on tight! We could be in for a showdown!"

Mischievous Itko ran up to Samson and stayed by his side. Taka just instinctively followed his brother while Washta watched helplessly as the wolves ran in tandem after the surprisingly unnerved buffalo.

"Do you think the wolves will attack the buffalo?" Michelle asked David.

"No, they won't," David said. "Taka and Itko have been raised in captivity. Plus, they are too young and all they want to do is play."

Buffalo Jones talked softly to Samson, "Good boy, Samson. Stay the course."

But Samson became excited with the wolves' company and decided to outrun them. He picked up his speed. The wolves kept up.

"Wow!" David said. "Samson is fast. This is so much fun!"

Samson was running full speed through the tall green and yellow grass of the prairie.

Buffalo Jones hung tight to the reins, hoping the buffalo wouldn't become so agitated by the presence of the wolves chasing him that he would decide to rear. That could be dangerous. He had seen him to do it a couple of times before.

Soon Taka tired, stopped, and stayed behind. Washta joined him a few minutes later and watched Itko disappear in the tall grass after Samson.

Itko came right up to Samson, who decided to show him he was superior. He was the king of the plains. He jumped straight up, confronting the unsuspecting, playful Itko.

"Whoa!" screamed Michelle in fear as David slid backward into her. "What's happening? We're going to die!"

"You won't," Buffalo Jones said. "I got you."

"Itko could die," David said. "But nothing is going to happen to us."

"Calm down. I've got everything under control," Buffalo Jones reassured them once more firmly.

Samson spooked Itko. Itko's ego deflated, he whimpered, turned around, and went back to Taka and Washta, who were walking toward Roosevelt. Roosevelt had seen the whole thing and was shaking his head in disbelief, preferring to stay put. He didn't want to stimulate Samson's temper any more than it was already.

Buffalo Jones, hanging on tightly to Michelle and David, quickly brought Samson under control.

A second later, the buffalo was calmly back on all fours, leaving the kids quite shaken up. David was still holding his magic coin tightly.

Samson stopped too and rested.

"Everything is going to be OK," Buffalo Jones said and smiled.

Michelle and David were still shaken by the showdown and the jump and couldn't utter a word.

"Samson, let's go back home," Buffalo Jones said, holding the reins tightly and riding Samson toward the tents. "Enough excitement for today."

"I am ready," Michelle said, relieved and letting out a big sigh.

"I'm not," David said. "That was so much fun." He loved the excitement and wished Buffalo Jones would keep on going.

25

Sitting Bull's Invitation

They rode back to where Roosevelt and Washta were, but Washta wasn't alone. David and Michelle recognized Washta's brother Kohona.

"Why do you think Kohona is here?" Michelle asked David. "Do you think Washta is in trouble?"

"He probably took too long to get back," David answered. "I'm sure they want to know if he saw buffalo."

"Or maybe they were upset to see him ride the buffalo," Michelle said. "The buffalo is sacred to them."

As they approached Washta and the wolves, they heard Washta ask Roosevelt if he would go meet Sitting Bull.

"My brother was sent here because I took too long in returning," Washta said. "But also Chief Sitting Bull would like to meet you and Buffalo Jones."

Michelle and David looked at each other, surprised. They had not seen Sitting Bull when they were there.

"Where do you think Sitting Bull was when we were in the dance circle?" Michelle asked.

"Who knows?" David answered. "Maybe he just arrived, or maybe he was the chief with the long headdress whose face we didn't see. Can you imagine? We are going to meet *Sitting Bull*."

"I can't believe it," Michelle said. "But do you think he's nice?"

"We'll find out soon enough," David said. "Remember he was fighting for his land. And Roosevelt and Buffalo Jones are on his land. So he may be curious why they are here."

"I know," Michelle said. "Mrs. Savant told us about his beliefs. Sitting Bull thought Indians should live freely on the land and that the government made promises that weren't kept. That's why I'm wondering if Sitting Bull will be nice to us."

Roosevelt approached Buffalo Jones to talk about the invitation to go across the river to talk to Sitting Bull.

"Not a problem," Buffalo Jones said, agreeing to meet Sitting Bull. "Hopefully, Sitting Bull is not upset with me riding a buffalo."

"He is probably very curious about seeing a man riding a buffalo," Roosevelt said. "He must think you have special power."

Roosevelt left Buffalo Jones and went to tell Kohona they would accept Sitting Bull's invitation.

As soon as he got the answer, Kohona left to tell Sitting Bull of their arrival.

26

Crossing the River on a Buffalo or in a Canoe?

Washta saw his brother leave and got ready to go himself.

"Why don't you ride in the canoe with me, Mr. Roosevelt?" Washta asked, inviting the young adventurer to join him.

"Sounds like a great idea," Roosevelt answered. He was looking forward to a canoe ride.

Roosevelt looked at Michelle and David and said, "Children, would you like to go across the river in the canoe with Washta and me?"

"Or would you like to stay with me and ride on Samson across the river?" Buffalo Jones asked.

Michelle couldn't wait to get off the buffalo, but she wanted to stay with David no matter what. So whatever David decided, she would go along.

David looked at Michelle. "How about we go with Buffalo Jones? It would be fun," David said.

"We have survived the prairie. What can happen in the river?"

"We're going to get wet," Michelle said, alarmed. "Worse, we could drown."

"I won't let that happen," David said confidently, touching his magic coin and trusting in its power.

"Yes," Buffalo Jones said. "You're going to get wet. Still want to do it?"

Michelle didn't want to get her red shoes wet but kept silent. She crossed her feet in front of her and made herself as small as possible.

"Sure! What's a little water?" David said, ebullient. He was always ready for an adventure. He stretched his legs straight up on the buffalo's neck.

Buffalo Jones realized that the kids didn't want to get wet, so he reached for the buffalo skin resting under the saddle and pulled it up to wrap Michelle's and David's bodies as best as he could.

"That should help a lot," Buffalo Jones said.

"I feel like I'm in a bag," Michelle said. "But it does stink," she whispered softly to David.

David shrugged his shoulder.

Roosevelt got in the canoe with Washta. Washta didn't wait for Buffalo Jones. They immediately left.

Buffalo Jones, Michelle, and David soon followed on Samson.

"Look! Everyone is at the shore," Michelle said, pointing at the huge crowd gathering to watch them go across the river.

"It looks like the whole village is here to greet us," David said.

"You guys ready?" Buffalo Jones asked. "Make sure you hang on tight to David, Michelle, and, David, hang on to the saddle."

"Aren't you going to hold us tight?" Michelle asked.

"Don't you worry," Buffalo Jones answered and smiled. "I got you good. Let's go take a bath, Samson."

And off they went into the calm river.

The massive buffalo got in, sprinkling water fifty feet out and sloshing.

"I feel like I'm in a banana boat, splashing water everywhere," David said, laughing. "I love it. Isn't it fun?"

"Kind of," Michelle said coolly and indifferently, not wanting to admit she was enjoying the ride, but she finally did relent, "Yes, it's much more fun than I thought it would be."

"Unbelievable," David said. "We're going across the river on the back of a buffalo. Who would have thought we would cross a river sitting on a buffalo?"

"You can't believe it?" Michelle said. "I can't believe it myself either."

The splashing and spattering had stopped.

"Now it feels like we're floating," Michelle said.

The composed buffalo was going across the water very slowly, making sure to keep his huge lion head above water. He was calm and very focused on the opposite side.

"Pretty smooth ride," Buffalo Jones said happily, proud of his buffalo.

"He likes the water," Michelle said, relaxing.

But then as they approached the shoreline, the buffalo lost his footing and took an unexpected dip. David, Michelle, and Buffalo Jones jerked forward.

The whole village screamed.

Washta turned around and saw the buffalo's head going into the water.

Buffalo Jones yanked David and Michelle back toward him.

"Everything is OK," Buffalo Jones said, reassuring the scared children. Just one of those unseen potholes. Samson is already getting his balance back."

"That was fun," David said, unnerved.

"How is Samson going to behave with all these people talking and screaming?" Michelle, still shaky, asked. She was a little skeptical about what could possibly happen once they reached the shoreline.

"Everything is going to be fine," Buffalo Jones reassured her.

Of course, the canoe was faster. Washta and Roosevelt got there first. Roosevelt waited in the canoe for Buffalo Jones and the children in case they needed quick rescuing.

Sitting Bull, followed by other chiefs and the medicine man, had come to greet this strange man riding a *tatanka* and his young mustached friend riding in a canoe.

The buffalo finally emerged from the water and slowly walked to shore to the excitement of all the children and the adults, who were fascinated by this man riding a buffalo as if it were a horse.

Michelle let out a big sigh of relief. "Finally on land!"

27

The Alligator Shoes and the Red Moccasins

The buffalo, under Buffalo Jones's gentle guidance, walked away from the crowd toward a quiet area, but the *tatanka* had a mind of its own and moved toward Sitting Bull and the medicine man. Buffalo Jones was powerless to change its course. It was like Samson was under a spell. No matter how hard he tried to make the buffalo go in a different direction, he couldn't.

The tatanka instinctively walked up to Sitting Bull and the medicine man. He dropped Buffalo Jones and the children right at Sitting Bull's feet as if he was giving Sitting Bull a gift.

"Who is this man whom the buffalo respects and allows to ride him?" Sitting Bull asked, looking curiously at this cool buffalo man.

"Why has the buffalo chosen to stop right here?" he continued, puzzled and perplexed, looking for a message sent by the Wakan Tanka.

Once more, Buffalo Jones tried to coax Samson to move, but he wouldn't budge one inch and stayed right there in front of Sitting Bull.

All the children rushed to see the amazingly docile buffalo, even though they had been told to stay out of the way because often buffalo could be dangerous. But this buffalo was different, and they wanted to see it up close and maybe even ride it just like the chief had done. But they were reined in by the medicine man, who turned to them and mumbled some strange words, which made them stop promptly.

"This man riding a buffalo must be very special and viewed highly by Wakan Tanka, the Great Spirit," the medicine man responded, turning back to Sitting Bull.

"I am Charlie Jesse *Buffalo* Jones," the buffalo man said and smiled nervously, getting off the powerful, serene, and dignified lion of the plains.

He wasn't sure how Sitting Bull and the chiefs would view his treatment of a buffalo, an animal they so honored.

"You have to tell us more about your buffalo," Sitting Bull said in a cordial manner.

"This is my trusted friend, Samson, and I treat him as such," Buffalo Jones answered, relaxing somewhat. "Samson wouldn't be interested in our meeting, so where would you suggest I put Samson while we talk for a bit? You understand I must go back on the trail in a few minutes. Samson likes to be in the open field, away from people. So will you allow me to tie him in a quiet area close by where he can rest away from all the noise? He is a bit tired after this water excursion."

"Certainly," Sitting Bull said, pointing to a post in front of them. "Why not here?"

Sitting Bull appreciated this caring attitude. He remained in place, observing the unusual man getting off the magnificent king of the plains, which was so unusually tame.

~

Roosevelt rushed to help the smiling children get off the buffalo. They were excited to see a very famous Indian, such as Sitting Bull, whom they had heard a lot about.

David touched his magic coin to make sure it was handy. *I have to be ready to use it just in case things heat up,* he thought.

Roosevelt, David, and Michelle stood silently, facing Samson, Sitting Bull, and the whole village. Washta soon joined them.

"Chief Sitting Bull, the man with the strange shoes is Theodore Roosevelt." Washta rushed to introduce his canoe companion, who was wearing a fringed buckskin shirt, a pearl-hilted revolver, and a silver-handled knife attached to his belt with a silver buckle.

Chief Sitting Bull walked up to Roosevelt and looked him all over; then he looked down at the strange-looking boots Roosevelt was wearing. Roosevelt followed his gaze.

"Very sturdy boots," Roosevelt said. "I need something dependable to ride and walk in the plains to fight the prickly plants and the snakes. These are made from the belly of an alligator."

"The man with the alligator boots has a special power," the medicine man announced. "He is a man of great understanding and will become a great mediator."

"I must show him the heart and the soul of our people," Sitting Bull told the medicine man.

"Make him see our pain at losing our land," the medicine man said to the silent, loving chief, who wanted nothing but happiness for his people and for them to live freely on their land as they had done for thousands of years.

The preoccupied chief heard the medicine man and kept silent for a few minutes.

"My moccasins are made with deer skin," the proud and reflective chief told Roosevelt, pointing at his red moccasins, which were decorated with blue and red beads, porcupine quills, and a picture of a black buffalo on top.

"The man with the alligator shoes has a special ability," the determined medicine man repeated.

Sitting Bull continued to glance at this man with a raccoon on his head.

"He is a man of great understanding," the medicine man prophesied. "He will talk with many nations and sign many treaties."

Roosevelt became pensive and smiled.

Michelle and David looked at each other. These things did happen. The medicine man could predict the future. Theodore Roosevelt would sign many treaties and become the most important man in the world, the twenty-sixth president of the United States.

But soon they became interested in the moment.

"Wow!" Michelle said, turning her attention to Sitting Bull's moccasins. "David, it's the first time I've seen red moccasins. Those are beautiful. Have you ever seen moccasins like that? Wouldn't it be fun to have red moccasins like that?"

"You only say that because you like the color red," David said, disinterested in footwear, no matter how colorful or fancy, like the alligator boots Roosevelt was wearing.

What intrigued David was whether Sitting Bull knew what an alligator was. Had Sitting Bull ever seen an alligator? If he hadn't, Sitting Bull never pursued the matter. Maybe in his travels, Sitting Bull had seen some.

Michelle and David had not paid attention to the alligator boots up until then; they had been too impressed by the man himself. But they now examined Roosevelt's boots and fancy silver buckle until they were called back to reality by Buffalo Jones's voice.

"Alligator boots and a silver belt buckle!" Michelle said. "I didn't know cowboys were fancy. I thought they were rough and simply dressed."

"Why not?'" David replied. "He is Teddy Roosevelt after all."

"Come, Samson; let's go," Buffalo Jones said.

Buffalo Jones tried again to nudge Samson to move, but he wouldn't. He stood paralyzed.

"Samson can be very stubborn at times," Buffalo Jones said, frustrated.

He checked the buffalo's hooves to make sure he hadn't injured himself in the sudden encounter with the pothole under the watchful eyes of Sitting Bull and his entourage. He then removed a leather satchel hanging on the side of the buffalo. He checked its contents.

"Good, the eggs are still intact and the flour and sugar are still dry," Buffalo Jones said, relieved to see his food staples safe. He needed those items to make bread for the road. But would he have time to bake it before resuming his travels? That would have to wait until later.

"Do you always carry eggs, flour, and sugar?" David asked.

"I do," Buffalo Jones answered. "I live on the road so I take my kitchen and staples with me."

He rubbed Samson's back.

"The hooves are fine," Buffalo Jones said, talking to Samson. "What's the problem? Why aren't you moving?" he continued patiently, not understanding this long pause.

"I know," Washta answered knowingly. "Samson wants to treat Sitting Bull to a ride on the prairie and share with the chief what it is to be riding a buffalo, roaming and galloping with the wind. He won't move unless Sitting Bull takes him to the prairie."

Sitting Bull had listened attentively to Washta and glanced at the medicine man.

"Maybe it is so," the medicine man said. "The buffalo is very generous and gives us all he has. But he has never shared his *alive* spirit. His presence here is very meaningful. Washta has been blessed with a vision, so I suggest you take advantage of riding a buffalo and go feel the wind as the buffalo feels it and wander through the prairie like he does. A revelation or his message will come upon you."

This was not what Buffalo Jones had in mind. He was hoping Samson would rest. He had swum across the river, and Roosevelt had ridden him at great length. Was Sitting Bull really interested in riding the buffalo? And if he did, how would Samson behave? Would the buffalo lose his calm composure? That was a lot of commotion in one day.

28

Sitting Bull's Buffalo Adventure

Buffalo Jones became very quiet and observed Samson for any unusual signs showing his disposition.

He wondered what would happen if Samson was spooked by Sitting Bull and started acting up. *It is one thing for me to ride him,* he thought. *I can always control him. Will the chief be angry with me if Samson loses his temper?*

"Let me ride this sacred buffalo," Sitting Bull said decisively, approaching the buffalo with a confident attitude. "Buffalo Jones, you can do it. So I will be able to."

"I'm sure you'll be as good a rider as I am, if not better," Buffalo Jones said, holding Samson's reins and hiding his discomfort. "Samson went to you. He must feel a connection. Let me help you up."

"I don't need your help," the illustrious chief said, trying unsuccessfully to hop onto the huge, undisturbed animal. He was hindered by his very long headdress.

Buffalo Jones retreated and decided to go see what was cooking. He always brought some flour, eggs, and sugar on his trips. *I am out of bread. Maybe this is the time to make some bread while I am here waiting for them to return*, he reckoned. He removed the bag containing the ingredients.

In the meantime, all the little kids thought it was funny to see their very important, great chief Sitting Bull trying to mount the buffalo. The placid buffalo was standing there without a reaction, not minding all the commotion about and around him.

"What a great buffalo!" David said.

Sitting Bull had no choice but to remove his many-feathered headdress, as it was in the way. He ceremoniously handed it to Washta, who had brought the buffalo to him and was standing by him.

"I will be very careful, Chief Sitting Bull," Washta said, honored to have been asked by the great chief.

Finally, after a few attempts, Sitting Bull was sitting in the buffalo's saddle, ready to ride into the prairie.

"Let me have the headdress," Sitting Bull demanded authoritatively. He never rode without it.

Washta handed the magnificent headdress back to Sitting Bull, who managed to put it back on his head as if it were weightless.

"I think you would be more comfortable without it," Buffalo Jones suggested as he was walking away.

"I ride horses with the headdress," Sitting Bull said, rejecting the proposition. "I will ride the buffalo with the headdress."

Just like a king, thought David. "A king is used to wearing his crown, and he would not want to do without it."

29

Sitting Bull's Demands Upset Michelle

David and Michelle were observing this well-known chief with intensity when without warning, Sitting Bull looked at David and said, "Come ride with me. I have something to show you, something you must see. You will be a leader one day, and you need to know."

"Me?" David asked with surprise. What would this important chief want to show him? The medicine man had told Sitting Bull that David was blessed by Wanka with the gift of going from one world to another to share his knowledge. Maybe he needed to bring a message from this world.

Roosevelt, seeing David's look of discomfort, interceded. "If you will allow me, I will take the child on one of your horses and follow you."

Sitting Bull thought for a minute and said, "Actually, this is a great idea. I can show you as well, and you can also convey to your people what my people are truly about."

Michelle shot a desperate look at David. *Where does that leave me? How about me?* Michelle thought. She didn't want to be left alone without him.

Sitting Bull looked at Michelle and said, "In that case, you, little girl, you ride with me. You can appreciate nature just as much as they can."

Michelle was scared of the chief, but what other choice did she have? The chief had spoken.

Hesitantly, she let herself be lifted onto the buffalo's saddle in front of Sitting Bull, who was sitting proudly with his back very straight and staring beyond the plains.

There she was one more time faced with having to ride the buffalo. But this time it wasn't the buffalo she was scared of.

Michelle was intimidated by this powerful chief, about whom she had heard so much.

"We are all set," David said, beaming. "I will be riding with Teddy Roosevelt, and you will be riding with Sitting Bull. A perfect situation. This is going to be so much fun."

"We'll see!" Michelle said with trepidation.

Washta brought a beautiful white horse whose blue saddle blanket was covered with vivid buffalo and eagle designs.

"Great-looking horse!" Roosevelt told Sitting Bull, admiring the majestic horse.

"Sunka-Wanka, Sacred Dog, is my best horse," Sitting Bull said proudly of his horse, who was painted with colorful designs. His mane was plaited with beads.

"Beautiful!" Michelle exclaimed. "I'd love to ride your horse."

Michelle was nervous to ride the buffalo with the Indian chief because she had heard he didn't like white people for what they had done to his people and his land. She was jealous at not being able to ride the horse. "I'd much rather ride the horse. Why do I ride the buffalo and you the horse?" she said to David.

"What's wrong with riding the buffalo with Sitting Bull?" David asked her, anxious to find out more about Roosevelt's handgun.

"You know I love riding horses," Michelle replied. "That's why."

Michelle thought, *Why does Sitting Bull want us to ride with him anyway?*

She wanted to ask David but was afraid to make matters worse for herself so she didn't. In any case, she couldn't; David was busy talking with Roosevelt about his silver revolver.

On his end, David was thrilled to be on a horse with the great Theodore Roosevelt and to go riding alongside Sitting Bull.

Just like Dad always says, David thought. *It's a win-win situation.*

"Let's go to the prairie," Sitting Bull ordered as the whole village watched in awe.

Sitting Bull started the buffalo very slowly. The buffalo walked obediently into the open grass, carrying out his command, followed by Roosevelt and David, who was much more comfortable than Michelle.

It's not fair, Michelle thought. *But I might as well try to enjoy this ride.*

Once they began moving, she felt the strong arms of Sitting Bull protecting her and she relaxed. All her fears disappeared mysteriously. She knew everything was going to be OK. There was more to Sitting Bull than his constant ferocious battle with the white people to preserve his land. She forgot all the mean things she had been told about him.

Still Michelle wondered, *What is on Sitting Bull's mind? What does he want to show us young kids?*

She was dying to know David's answer to that. He would know. She looked at David again, but he was now busy talking to Roosevelt about his favorite horse, Manitou. Sitting Bull was right there, so it would be hard for him to answer anyway. Michelle kept quiet and listened.

"Manitou is surefooted," Roosevelt said. "I can leave him in one spot, and he will be happy to stay there grazing for a long while. That's why I am confident he will stay by the campsite's tent until I return."

30

Sitting Bull's Message

∽

It didn't take long to find out what Sitting Bull had in mind.

They all rode peacefully and quietly for a few minutes.

"For thousands of years, we were born free to wander through this beautiful land, living peacefully with millions of buffalo roaming, free to be totally self-sufficient because the buffalo gave us everything we needed to live so free and to love life," Sitting Bull said sadly, pointing at all that surrounded them. "And now look around; there is not one buffalo to be found on a land destroyed of its natural resources. My people are starving. What will happen to us if we don't fight to save our land and our way of life?"

Michelle and David knew the answer and were sad. Mrs. Savant had talked about the fate of the starving Indians on reservations.

"I admire Buffalo Jones," Sitting Bull said, continuing to the river. "He treats the buffalo with respect, as something special Mother Earth gave him, just like my people do. From the beginning of time, we have lived in harmony and peace with all the animals. We kill them only when we need food, but we pray, asking them permission to kill them and then we ask forgiveness. Sadly, our lives have changed. Our hunting way of life is no more. We are no longer free."

Roosevelt listened attentively. He too hunted for food, but he also hunted to learn about the animal's behavior. He also knew that sometimes even the Indians killed far more buffalo than they needed. They were human, just like everyone else.

Yes, the Indians' respect for nature and attitude toward the land was unparalleled, but ways of life were changing and nothing could stop progress. Roosevelt hoped that wisdom would guide the Indians in a new direction. From the beginning of time, there had been wars; people had fought, lost their land, and survived, and so would the Indians, he was sure.

Sitting Bull came to an oak tree and stopped. He then looked at Roosevelt and said, "I have been offered money for my land, our people's land. I will never sell nor allow the trees along the river to be cut down. Our nation believes that everything Mother Earth gives us is sacred. White men don't think like us."

Sitting Bull stopped talking and closed his eyes. Everything was very quiet.

Roosevelt, David, and Michelle listened to the sounds of nature. Even though David and Michelle were children, they wanted to feel what Sitting Bull was communicating to them. They had heard about the fate of the Native Americans from Mrs. Savant and read about it in books.

Pointing at the oak tree, Sitting Bull said, "I cherish the oak tree because its acorn is incredibly telling." He continued. "The acorn is a sacred seed. It contains life within, yet it is invisible. It endures the winter storms and the heat of summer, like our nation endures, develops, and blooms. If one cuts down the oak tree, there will be no acorns and no more oak trees. What will our nation become?

Again, Sitting Bull became silent.

David and Michelle weren't sure what to say or do.

Then, Sitting Bull started singing, "Young men help me. I love my nation so that's why I am fighting."

Sitting Bull approached the oak tree, picked up a handful of acorns, and gave them to Michelle and David.

"Remember, there is life in everything. Everything has a spirit, even though invisible to the eye," Sitting Bull said. "So, we must respect all living things."

"Even if the living things are our enemies," Michelle said out loud without thinking.

"Yes, and it's hard to love your enemies when they break their promises," Sitting Bull said. "I am a peace-loving man, and I will not fight unless provoked. Sadly, many white men have come and promised to leave us and our land alone, but these promises have been broken. I fight passionately with my words, but I will fight with blood to survive. There is a saying that if one can touch an enemy rather than kill him, he is a man of honor. Others have fought to the blood. I would rather touch an enemy than kill him. I am a man of honor before all else. I keep hoping that there will be no more fighting and that someone will listen to us."

Michelle and David were heavy-hearted. They knew what would happen to the Native Americans.

They kept their silence for a bit and then said, "Wopila tanka," politely accepting the acorns.

31

David's Gift to Sitting Bull

David instinctively looked in his pockets for something to give the famous chief. He couldn't find anything really worth giving to an important chief, such as Sitting Bull, except the gray dove feather he had found in front of the American History Museum.

As they were riding close to one another, David grabbed the gray feather, stretched out his arm, and said, "Chief Sitting Bull, I have something for you."

Sitting Bull, surprised by the offering, looked at David. He was about to accept the feather when he stretched too far out and yanked the rein. The buffalo thought that meant for him to go faster so he took off at a full gallop. Sitting Bull fell sideways and hung there for a few seconds, scaring Michelle.

Michelle closed her eyes and held her breath. "Oh no!" she said.

But in some mysterious way, as if Sitting Bull had been pulled back by a strange power, he was now sitting erect, acting calm and collected like nothing had happened.

The gray feather floated and landed at just the right place—on the Indian chief's chest.

Sitting Bull looked at the feather, and his great laugh echoed loudly through the open plain.

"Wopila tanka, thank you, David, with all my heart for your gentle act of kindness," Sitting Bull said, still laughing. "I appreciate this greatly."

"I know you are a great chief and my gift is very small," David said, uncomfortable. "But all I have of value is this little gray feather."

"The gift of a feather is very meaningful," Sitting Bull said. "Do you know about the importance of feathers in our way of life?"

"Not really," David answered.

"The feather is a gift from the birds in the sky," Sitting Bull said. "Birds bring messages. Because the feathers are part of the bird, the feathers are meant to guide and protect. The feathers from different birds have their own meaning, even this little dove's feather. The dove's feathers symbolize gentleness and kindness. So I thank you for the gift."

"Even if I found the feather on the ground?" David asked, unsure if it was less meaningful because he had picked it up from the ground.

"Yes," Sitting Bull answered. "Finding a feather is a sign that you will have protection in what you do."

David smiled. It was true. He had been and had felt safe in his travel to Washta's village where Native American ways of life were changing.

Sitting Bull was touched by the little boy's kindness and generosity. This little white boy had more presence of mind than any of the government officials he had met so far.

32

Itko Teases Samson

"Look," Michelle said, pointing to Itko, who was chasing a rabbit a few feet away. "Itko got away again."

"Itko, come back here!" shouted Washta, running after him.

"Let him be," Sitting Bull said. "He is doing what he should be doing...He was born to run free."

"I know, but I am afraid he will get too close to Samson!" Washta yelled, trying to stop Itko. "I am trying to protect you."

"Don't worry," Sitting Bull said. "Tanka is looking over us."

So without restraint, Itko approached the buffalo one more time. The buffalo remembered him and started running faster toward the campsite.

"There we go, Samson, good son," Sitting Bull said, holding the reins tightly as the buffalo ran full speed ahead toward Buffalo Jones and the village, paying attention to nothing in his way.

They arrived safely at the campsite to the sounds of drums and the shouts of joy of everyone present. Samson slowed down, out of breath, and walked on sluggishly.

The camp was small, as everyone had been forced to live on a reservation. Sitting Bull had defied the orders to go live on a reservation, and so had some of his followers.

I would love my people to be free like this, happy to live where they choose, Sitting Bull thought. *I will never surrender.*

Sitting Bull refused to have anything to do with the demands of the white man that they change their ways of life by giving up their land to live on reservations. He was not going to live on a reservation like so many others had since 1868. So, he and some of his followers continued to live freely where they wanted, as their ancestors had done since the beginning of time.

33

What's Buffalo Jones Doing Cooking with the Women?

"Chief, let us ride the tatanka with you?" pleaded the excited children surrounding Sitting Bull.

"The tatanka is tired," the wise Sitting Bull said, getting slowly off the buffalo, keeping his headdress on his head. "Let's let him rest, and then we will see."

"Where is Buffalo Jones?" Michelle asked as Sitting Bull lifted her down.

"Look! He is with the women," Sitting Bull answered.

"Is he cooking?" Michelle asked, surprised to see him busy at the fire pits, surrounded by Indian women. She thought, *What does Sitting Bull think about Buffalo Jones cooking?*

Roosevelt and David were already off Sitting Bull's white horse, waiting to see what was expected of them.

~

Washta, followed by Itko and Taka, came to David and Roosevelt, who was busy tending to Sitting Bull's horse.

"David, are you hungry?" Washta asked.

"Yes," David said.

David was always hungry. "But first, let's get Michelle."

They both approached Sitting Bull and Michelle, who were walking toward the fire pits where Buffalo Jones and a few curious women stood cooking and talking. Buffalo Jones was busy turning pieces of meat lying on green leaves over a fire.

"It smells good," Michelle said.

"I am so hungry," David said.

"What is she cooking?" Michelle asked, pointing at Wise Owl, who was stirring something in a bag hanging over a fire. Michelle did not know that the bag was the stomach of a buffalo.

"Buffalo stew," Washta answered.

~

"What's happening here?" Sitting Bull asked, looking over at the meat lying on top of the green leaves.

"We are busy stirring turnips, wild onions, corn, and chunks of buffalo meat," Wise Owl said, uncomfortable with Sitting Bull's displeased tone of voice.

She ignored Sitting Bull's question about what Buffalo Jones was cooking. She knew Sitting Bull was asking about Buffalo Jones. A man never cooked in a Lakota village. It was a woman's job.

"I know you are, but what is he doing?" Sitting Bull asked. "He is not using a buffalo stomach to protect the meat from dirt."

Wise Owl kept her eyes down, afraid to incense the big chief more.

"Yuck! A buffalo stomach!" Michelle whispered in David's ear. "I don't think I want to eat the buffalo stew now, even though it smells good."

"I am grilling," Buffalo Jones answered. "This is very new to the women here. They told me they always boil or roast their meat. And don't worry; grilling the meat over leaves has been done for a long time, and people have never gotten sick."

"I don't want to change our ways," Sitting Bull said.

"I am not trying to change your ways," Buffalo Jones said. "Grilling is the only way I know to cook."

"Don't the Lakota barbecue?" Michelle asked. "It would seem so easy since they cook over a fire all the time."

"Michelle!" David said, looking exasperated at Michelle's continuous allusions to a different time.

"What?" Michelle replied. "The Taino Indians barbecued in the sixteenth century, so how do you know the Lakota didn't or don't?"

"The Taino Indians are not related to the Lakota," David replied, sure of himself. "They lived across the ocean a long way from here."

"We have been boiling or drying our meat for hundreds of years," Sitting Bull said, a little annoyed at the white man's way of cooking. "That's the way we like it."

"It's very simple to grill the meat the way Buffalo Jones is," said Wise Owl, finally taking her courage in her hands. "It could be useful. Why don't we try it?" She added, "We could do this kind of cooking when on the move by just putting a few leaves on a fire and grilling whatever we catch."

"We, the Lakota, are not going to change our ways," Sitting Bull told Wise Owl in a firm voice.

"It smells great," David said.

Sitting Bull, preoccupied, watched in silence.

"What are you grilling?" David asked Buffalo Jones.

"A squirrel," Buffalo Jones answered. "Itko brought it to us."

"Yuck!" Michelle exclaimed. "Squirrel...I am not having squirrel."

Michelle then turned to David and whispered again, "Cooking meat in a buffalo stomach and now a squirrel...I think I would die of hunger if I lived here."

"It's very yummy," Buffalo Jones, who had overheard Michelle, said. "Have you ever eaten squirrel?"

"No," Michelle said, refusing to look at the pieces of squirrel lying on the fire. "They're too cute."

"You don't know what you're missing," Sitting Bull said. He had relaxed a little. "You will have to try a little bite later on."

"OK," Michelle, not wanting to be impolite, said in a very soft voice.

"Isn't there some other meats there?" David asked. "These look different." He pointed at two other strips of meat.

"These are buffalo and elk strips," Buffalo Jones answered.

"That's better," Michelle said, happy to see there was some buffalo meat not being cooked in a buffalo stomach.

"What is Wise Owl doing with the little balls?" David asked.

"She is—" Buffalo Jones started to say.

"I am dropping them in grease...bear grease," Wise Owl said. "I am making fried corn bread for Buffalo Jones so he can take it on his travels."

In silence, Sitting Bull watched Wise Owl make fried breads and Buffalo Jones grill buffalo meat.

34

Sitting Bull Grills Buffalo Jones

What was the great chief thinking?

Seeing the famous chief pensive, Washta asked, “Sitting Bull, isn’t Samson great fun?”

“Yes, Samson is a great giver,” Sitting Bull said, and turning to Buffalo Jones, he seriously asked, “Do you intend to always ride the buffalo?”

“I intend to keep him for as long as he wants to be part of my life,” Buffalo Jones said. “I like buffalo, and I feel bad that there are only a few left. I am planning to bring them back by raising them.”

“Noble,” Sitting Bull said thoughtfully.

Michelle didn’t want to be rude and was waiting patiently to be dismissed by Sitting Bull, who quickly realized it.

“Washta, why don’t you show David and Michelle—” Sitting Bull couldn’t finish his sentence, as the playful Itko ran up to him and deposited at his feet a lively rabbit he had just found.

"Should I grill this one too?" Buffalo Jones asked, laughing and watching the rabbit escape.

Sitting Bull laughed. "No need to."

Everyone joined in the laughter.

Itko, unhappy to see the rabbit escape, rushed to retrieve it. He ran quickly before someone or another animal grabbed the rabbit away from him.

"Come back here, Itko!" Washta yelled.

Itko didn't listen and immediately disappeared behind the tepees. As usual, Itko was being Itko.

Washta and Taka ran after him.

35

Will Michelle Eat Buffalo Cooked in a Buffalo's Stomach?

"Come with me," Washta said to David and Michelle. "Let's go see where Itko is going."

David and Michelle followed Washta and Taka.

Itko had stopped by a warm fire where more women were cooking food.

"It smells good here too," Michelle said, eyeing the food. "I hope I smell buffalo and not squirrel."

Washta laughed and said, "It's buffalo."

A friendly little girl named Swift Feet approached Michelle and David. "Here is some pemmican."

David quickly grabbed the pemmican and chewed it. "Not bad," he said. "What do you think, Michelle?"

"What is pemmican?" Michelle asked, eyeing the brown ball she was holding.

"Oh! Don't worry about what it is," David said. "Just put it in your mouth and chew it like chewing gum."

"Who knows? It could be squirrel," Michelle said disdainfully. "Unless you tell me, I am not putting this pemmican in my mouth."

"Oh! Try a little bit," David insisted. "You will be surprised at the taste. You'll like it."

"Frankly, I'm not hungry," Michelle said.

"Pemmican is dried buffalo mixed with berries," Swift Feet said.

Taka came to David, begging for a little of his pemmican, but David had put the whole thing in his mouth.

Michelle, uncertain whether she should take a bite of the pemmican, was still looking at it when Taka jumped on it and stole the piece from her.

"Saved," David said, laughing and watching Taka chew the pemmican with gusto.

"Taka, what did you do?" Washta said.

"Now you will never know what it tastes like," David told Michelle.

Itko, jealous, wanted a piece too and went after Taka to steal his.

Wise Owl came to Washta and softly said, "Sitting Bull is asking for you and your friends to join him, as they are about to eat."

No one had seen Wise Owl approach them.

"Great," Washta said. "We are all starving. Let's go eat."

"OK," David said.

Michelle didn't say anything. She wasn't looking forward to eating food cooked in a buffalo's stomach.

"Have you ever had buffalo stew?" Washta asked.

"Never," David and Michelle said in unison.

"Does it taste like beef?" Michelle asked.

"I think buffalo tastes better," Washta said. "It is not stringy like cow meat."

"I can't wait," David said.

Again, Michelle didn't say anything. If she could help it, she wouldn't eat buffalo cooked in a stomach.

36

Will Sitting Bull Eat What Buffalo Jones Cooked?

They walked up to Sitting Bull, who was sitting in a circle surrounded by a small group of Native Americans and, of course, Roosevelt and Buffalo Jones.

"*Wakanisha,* children. Come and sit by my side," said Sitting Bull, holding a calumet and pointing at the three empty spots on his right. Sitting Bull loved children and was happy to share a Lakota meal with them.

"It is sad that you have missed the pipe ceremony. We prayed for peace and for the well-being of the visiting strangers," Sitting Bull said seriously. "But you are just in time to share Lakota food, which is another of our important ways."

"I am so sorry we missed the pipe ceremony," David said sincerely. "We have never seen one."

"I am sorry you missed it too. Still you need to remember the calumet is a needed to communicate our goal for peace," Sitting Bull said. "The pipe is a link between the earth and the sky. The smoke from the pipe carries our prayer up to the Great Spirit, Wakan Takan. It is a way to remember and show respect for Wakan Takan, respect for Mother Earth, respect for our fellow men and women, and respect for individual freedom. Only with respect will there be positive changes and peace in the world."

Michelle and David were very attentive to the big chief's words. This explanation was new to them.

"Now, I understand what the peace pipe is all about," David said in awe.

"I have seen pictures of a calumet," Michelle said. "But I had never seen a real one."

"Well, come close and take a look," Sitting Bull said, impressed by the enthusiasm for his culture demonstrated by the two children in front of him.

Michelle, David, and even Washta approached Sitting Bull. They listened attentively as Sitting Bull told of the calumet.

"The bowl of the calumet is made of a red stone to symbolize earth, and the buffalo standing on the bowl represents all four-legged animals," Sitting Bull said, pointing to the red bowl.

"It's a beautiful stone," David said. "You know I collect stones, but I have none like this one."

"We get the stone from a sacred place," Sitting Bull said. "The legend has it that the red stone is made from the flesh and blood of our ancestors. Unfortunately, there is no red stone around."

"Maybe I can find a little one for you," Washta said.

"The stem represents all that grows on earth," Sitting Bull continued. "The feathers represent all the winged things."

"Do you smoke the pipe every day?" Michelle asked.

"No," Sitting Bull answered, putting the pipe on the ground very carefully in front of him on top of a buckskin pipe bag.

"I wish I could take a calumet home," David whispered to Michelle.

"That would be nice, I know," Michelle said and smiled.

David, Michelle, and Washta went to sit on the right side of Sitting Bull. Roosevelt and Buffalo Jones were on the left side, drinking tea.

"This is beautiful," Michelle whispered to David, touching the buffalo hide they were sitting on and mesmerized by all the drawings. "There are all kinds of colorful designs. Look at the buffalo, the sun, and the tepees."

"The drawings tell our history," Sitting Bull said proudly. "The history of the Lakota."

Sitting Bull said a prayer, thanking the Great Spirit for nature and its goodness in all the food that they were about to eat.

Wise Owl brought the buffalo stew and served it first to Sitting Bull, who always sat on the ground because he wanted to be closer to Mother Earth.

Sitting Bull took his bowl, closed his eyes, and reopened them. He poured some of his soup stew into both Roosevelt's and Buffalo Jones's bowls.

When Washta saw this, he decided to do the same. He shared his stew with David and Michelle.

"I like the bowl," Michelle said.

"It is made from the buffalo horn," Washta said.

"Wow!" Michelle said. "The buffalo does give you everything."

"Thank you, Sitting Bull, for sharing this meal with all of us," Roosevelt said, thoroughly enjoying his first homemade Lakota meal.

"This is very good," David said, eating the buffalo stew with gusto.

Wise Owl hesitantly brought the grilled meats to the big chief.

"Sitting Bull, please try this grilled buffalo," Wise Owl said softly. "Buffalo Jones showed us how to grill. We would like to know if you like it as much as we did, even though this new way of cooking will not stop us from cooking the way our ancestors did."

Sitting Bull hesitantly took the grilled meat on a stick, looked at it, and took a bite, even though doing so was to accept the white man's way of doing things. He didn't want to show disrespect to his guest, so he ate the whole grilled piece.

"This is good," Sitting Bull said approvingly to Wise Owl's relief and happiness.

Wise Owl was pleased to see Sitting Bull's reaction.

"I am glad you enjoy my cooking, Sitting Bull," Buffalo Jones said. "I travel many miles with myself as the only company, so I need to cook in order to survive. This is the best way I know how."

"How about you, Mr. Roosevelt?" Sitting Bull asked. "Do you grill meats?"

"Yes, sometimes, but I'm not as good as Buffalo Jones," Roosevelt answered, stuttering. "I have to admit that I have help at the ranch with the cooking. I was on my way back to the ranch when I got stuck in a storm and met Buffalo Jones, who made me his special wild turkey soup."

"Can we go with you to your ranch?" Michelle asked, interrupting Roosevelt.

"The ranch?" Sitting Bull asked.

"Yes," Roosevelt answered. "I have a place called Chimney Butte Ranch a few miles from here with some cattle. Sitting Bull, I would love for you to come and see it."

37

Under Attack

They heard *ping, ping, poomb, poomb* in the distance.

Sitting Bull didn't have time to comment. He was quickly on his feet, as was everyone else, and called his men to follow him.

"What's going on?" David asked, sitting down and watching all the frenetic activity around.

"Are these gunshots?" Michelle asked, looking around nervously.

"Yes," Roosevelt said, calmly standing up.

Buffalo Jones and Washta got up too, evaluating the situation.

More rifle shots sounded.

Pandemonium ensued. Everyone was screaming and rushing in every direction. Shots were coming closer.

Sitting Bull ran to his horse, jumped on it, and rushed out in the direction of the shots fired, and so did the other men.

"Here, take this bag," Washta said as he removed the little buckskin bag shaped like a turtle from his neck. "You will find what you were wishing for."

"Wopila Tanka, Washta," David said, opening the bag and finding a little calumet made with the sacred red stone.

"A calumet!" David said with incredible joy. "Are you sure you can give me this?"

"I am sure," Washta said. "I must go find my father."

He quickly disappeared behind the tepees where the men were leaving on their horses making a dust storm in their haste.

"Are we being attacked?" Michelle asked, frozen in place, blinded by the clouds of dust.

"I don't know," Roosevelt said authoritatively to the children. "But we need to leave immediately. Come with me. Let's find Manitou and head on to Chimney Butte to join my men, who are cowboying."

"*Cowboying*!" David said, beaming. "Cowboying, that's a cool word. How fun! I can't wait."

"How about *stagecoaching*?" Michelle asked excited, trying to come up with a big word too.

"Quite possible," Roosevelt answered, laughing.

38

The Magic Coin

Michelle and David had forgotten all about the museum.

David took his coin out of his pocket, grasped Michelle's hand, and whispered to the coin.

About the Book

This is an educational historical novel for kids, ages nine and up. It is based on facts mixed with whimsical fiction. The goal is to teach kids history while making it fun.

See you at Theodore Roosevelt's Chimney Butte Ranch!

—David and Michelle

I hope you enjoyed the first book of the America series.

Let me know at paulinedesaintjustg@aol.com.

Pauline de Saint-Just Gross

Author's Note

Sitting Bull: Champion of the Sioux by Stanley Vestal- https://books.google
Manataka.org- Sitting Bull by Christiane Whiteswan Sterne
Lakotaperspectives.com,-Sitting Bull by Janis Schmidt

~

Indian Calumet: The Pipe of Peace by Christopher Nyerges

~

Legends of America.com
Moeurs et histoire des peaux rouges, https://classiques.uqac
Myths and legends of the Sioux, https://web.archive.org
Facts for Kids, Sioux Indians, www.bigorrin.org/sioux

If you have questions about specific historical material, email me and I'll do my best to answer.
paulinedesaintj@aol.com

Leonardo da Vinci, Columbus and
Little David
Written by
Pauline de Saint-Just Gross

Michelangelo, Columbus and
Little David
Written by
Pauline de Saint-Just Gross

Henry VII, Prince Arthur, Columbus
and Little David
Written by
Pauline de Saint-Just Gross

Anne of Brittany,
Arnaud the Page, Columbus and
Little David
Written by
Pauline de Saint-Just Gross

Isabella of Spain, Boabdil, Columbus and
Little David
Written by
Pauline de Saint-Just Gross

Made in the USA
San Bernardino, CA
10 October 2017